DEATH IN DESOLATION

George Bellairs (1902–1982). He was, by day, a Manchester bank manager with close connections to the University of Manchester. He is often referred to as the English Simenon, as his detective stories combine wicked crimes and classic police procedurals, set in quaint villages.

He was born in Lancashire and married Gladys Mabel Roberts in 1930. He was a devoted Francophile and travelled there frequently, writing for English newspapers and magazines and weaving French towns into his fiction.

Bellairs' first mystery, *Littlejohn on Leave* (1941) introduced his series detective, Detective Inspector Thomas Littlejohn. Full of scandal and intrigue, the series peeks inside small towns in the mid twentieth century and Littlejohn is injected with humour, intelligence and compassion.

He died on the Isle of Man in April 1982 just before his eightieth birthday.

ALSO BY GEORGE BELLAIRS

The Case of the Famished Parson
The Case of the Demented Spiv
Corpses in Enderby
Death in High Provence
Death Sends for the Doctor
Murder Makes Mistakes
Bones in the Wilderness
Toll the Bell for Murder
Death in the Fearful Night
Death in the Wasteland
Death of a Shadow
Intruder in the Dark
Death in Desolation
The Night They Killed Joss Varran

DEATH IN DESOLATION

GEORGE BELLAIRS

ipso books

This edition published in 2016 by Ipso Books

First published in 1967 in Great Britain by John Gifford Ltd.

Ipso Books is a division of Peters Fraser + Dunlop Ltd

Drury House, 34-43 Russell Street, London WC2B 5HA

Copyright © George Bellairs, 1967

All rights reserved

You may not copy, distribute, transmit, reproduce or otherwise make available this publication (or any part of it) in any form, or by any means (including without limitation electronic, digital, optical, mechanical, photocopying, printing, recording or otherwise), without the prior written permission of the publisher. Any person who does any unauthorised act in relation to this publication may be liable to criminal prosecution and civil claims for damages.

Contents

The Farmhouse Crimes	1
A Round of Town	16
The Confidences of Harry Quill	26
Legal Opinion	39
The Rat Race	52
Stillwaters	68
Gathering of the Clan	80
Cromwell among the Mourners	99
Quill's Last Day	114
Treasure Hunt	132
Prosecution and Defence	145
Trial and Error	158
Order out of Confusion	173
The Night They Killed Joss Varran	189

CHAPTER I
THE FARMHOUSE CRIMES

It could almost be said that Littlejohn got involved in the Farmhouse Murders by accident.

Throughout the spring and summer of 1965 the newspaper headlines were monopolised by a series of carefully planned crimes in farmhouses in remote areas. The first occurred in Devonshire; the next in the Lake District; then in the Yorkshire Dales. Each crime greatly distant from the last and the whole country wondering where the next would happen.

The robberies were committed with a minimum of violence. In most cases the victims were surprised at night, threatened, tied-up and gagged with transparent tape and their cash...nothing but cash...carried off. Once or twice, when the occupant showed resistance or lack of co-operation, he was hit over the head.

The criminals had obviously made their plans carefully in advance. They appeared mainly on local mart days, which terminated after the banks had closed and left farmers with cash in hand from cattle deals. There were three operators and they never tackled any place with more than three people on the premises. The raiders had been carefully described over and over again from the start, but the details were of little help. They all wore black nylon stockings over their heads and faces, with black gloves on their hands and rope-soled slippers of the foreign *espadrille* type on their feet.

They were a quick-moving lot. If there was a telephone to the place they visited, they cut the outside wires beforehand. If the farmer had a shotgun handy, one of them, who might have been a gymnast or a rugby player, was upon him in a flying tackle before he could use it. On one occasion only, when the victim had been too quick for the athlete, one of his companions had drawn a revolver and persuaded the farmer to hand over his own weapon. The leader was tall, thin and lithe, and attended to his business with speed and concentration; another, stocky and powerful, intent on overcoming scruples and resistance; the third was described as self-confident, almost cocky, a youngish man, nimble, slim and of medium height, who seemed to creep more than walk in a slimy sadistic way. They were all dressed in black trousers and sweaters and became known as the Black Lot.

After the unsolved sixth crime in Pembrokeshire, there was a terrific public outcry. Half the police of the country and most of the men in rural areas were out after them, but nobody could pretend to guard every isolated farmhouse against the intruders. Everybody was, as usual, asking what the police were doing about it, especially after the seventh crime, when The Creep, as the youngest of the trio had been called, shot and badly wounded a farmer who refused to be intimidated and snatched at his mask. Then only had the leader lost his temper and struck his companion a vicious blow across the mouth with the back of his gloved hand.

The police work had already been centralised under a Devonshire Superintendent, Warlock, who had taken charge of the first of the investigations and whose energy and intelligence, although hitherto unsuccessful, had attracted the attention of his superiors. He had worked night and day until his efforts were cut short by a coronary attack which placed him in hospital for the rest of the summer. There, he received flowers with a 'Get Better Quickly' card on which were stuck with transparent tape four words clipped from a newspaper: *from the black lot.*

It was then that Littlejohn was appointed co-ordinator of the enquiry, and Cromwell was assigned to assist him.

Almost at once another crime, this time murder, was reported, at Sprawle Corner, a remote hamlet, near Marcroft, in Midshire.

When Littlejohn and Cromwell got out of the train at Rugby, Cromwell looked distastefully round the station.

'An aunt of mine, the black sheep of the family, once ran off with a porter she met on Rugby station and was never seen again,' he said, as if to himself.

There wasn't time for further details. Someone pushed his way through the crowd and dashed up to Cromwell.

'Chief Superintendent Littlejohn? I recognised you right away from your photos in the paper. My name's Crampitt, sir. Sergeant in the Midshire C.I.D. I've been sent to meet you. Rugby's not exactly in our manor and if the local boys had known you were coming, they'd have had the red carpet out...'

He cordially wrung Cromwell's hand and looked expectantly at Littlejohn, waiting to be introduced.

Littlejohn had difficulty in taking it seriously. Cromwell had to put his hand heavily on Crampitt's shoulder to stop the gush of his welcome.

'*This* is Chief Superintendent Littlejohn. My name's Cromwell.'

Crampitt wasn't in the least put out. He was young and resilient and wore a natty dark grey suit and a jaunty cloth hat with a feather in the band. He removed the hat and revealed a crew cut.

'I must have got you both mixed up. You were both in the picture in the paper, weren't you? This way.'

He led them through the milling crowds of travellers to a car standing in the forecourt of the station.

'Superintendent Taylor asked me to come and meet you both. He's been detained on the Sprawle Corner murder. He'll be glad to see you. Superintendent Warlock was in charge of the farm crime cases, but his heart attack put an end to that. He's still on the sick list and we're having to improvise a bit...'

He had relieved them of their luggage and rammed it in the boot of the police car, still talking. They all climbed in the vehicle.

The sun was shining and the streets of Rugby were full of shoppers and cars. Crampitt drove quickly, but that didn't prevent his talking. Littlejohn filled and lit his pipe and Crampitt apparently took this as permission to smoke himself. After pulling up at traffic lights, he rapidly produced a small cheroot for himself and another for Cromwell and lit them both before the lights changed to green. The car filled with the opulent smell of cigars.

'We'll take the road through the country to Marcroft. It passes Sprawle. The scenery's nice, too.'

They might have been going on a picnic.

'Perhaps I'd better tell you a bit about the case, sir...'

He took the silence as consent and although they were travelling at sixty he rattled off his tale, speaking round the cheroot.

'Sprawle Corner's a strange place. There are three farms there and four houses and a Methodist chapel, all unoccupied, except one, Great Lands, where the dead man and his wife lived. His name was Quill.'

Crampitt coughed, opened the window and flung away his half-smoked cheroot impatiently as though it were choking him.

'The Quills were a queer lot. I was born not far from Sprawle and know about them. Harry Quill, the murdered man, was the last of the older generation and the last of the family who farmed Great Lands for centuries. He'd no children and I suppose his three nephews will inherit the farm, such as it is.'

'It's not much of a place, then?'

'Five hundred acres...'

'Not bad.'

'It *is* bad, though. Harry Quill was off his head. There were three farms there: Great Lands, with three hundred acres, and two others with about a hundred acres apiece. One of the small holdings was farmed by a chap called Seal; the other by a man of the name of Russell. A tractor overturned and killed Seal; Russell got drinking and went bust. Quill bought both farms, added the land to his own and let the farmhouses go derelict. The doors and anything else portable were soon pinched, the windows were all broken by hooligans and somebody even took slates off the roofs. The two farmhouses and a tied cottage that went with Isaac Seal's holding are just skeletons in ruins now.'

'But Quill farmed his five hundred acres?'

'That's just it. He didn't. He simply bought the two hundred acres and left them as they were – plus more than two hundred acres of his own. Almost the whole of the farm he allowed to go back to the wild.'

'Had he no stock?'

'A few sheep in the fields surrounding the house, that's all. The local agricultural committee took it up. They threatened what they'd do if he didn't put the land under cultivation again or else stock it, but they didn't seem to get very far. I don't know why. When you visit the farm, you'll see where all the five hundred acres, which had been salvaged from moorland at one time, are reverting to moorland again. You can see the wilderness encroaching like the tide coming in.'

He paused as though admiring his metaphors.

'What kind of a man was Harry Quill?'

'He was always odd and a bit of a recluse. A middle-sized man, fattish, with a red, clean shaven face when he *did* shave, and a shock of thick grey hair which looked as if it had never seen a comb. He always looked as if he'd robbed a scarecrow in his style of dress. No collar, a brass stud in the neckband of his shirt, and old clothes. He used to run into Marcroft now and then to do some shopping. He was always alone. His wife was an invalid. I heard she'd had polio when she was young and walked like somebody who'd had a stroke. She was Harry Quill's cousin and it's said he married her to keep the money in the family.'

'Was there money in the family, then?'

'That's a puzzle. After the murder, we had to go through the place and all the cash we found – his lawyer was with us to make matters regular – all the cash we found was about three pounds, four and ninepence halfpenny... I remember the halfpenny...'

'What had Mrs. Quill to say about it?'

'Not a thing. It seems Quill looked after all the money. With her being confined indoors, she never needed any cash and he never gave her any. There was no cheque book or bank passbook, no sign of invested savings... nothing. He either buried his cash or hid it in some safe place, or else the robbers found it and took it off with them. He used to pay his bills in cash and bought and sold odd items of stock now and then, so he must have had cash available more than we found...'

They arrived at a signpost which pointed from the trunk road to a narrower one. *Sprawle and Marcroft.*

The gradient gradually began to increase almost as soon as they left the highway and they snaked their way upwards to an acute corner with another sign: *Sprawle. Cul-de-sac.* They turned into a well-made road in which, however, two cars could only have passed with difficulty. Ditches along each side and tall bushes which cut off the view. Finally, the hedges thinned out and revealed the deserted hamlet which the murdered man, pursuing some crazy policy known only to himself, had denuded of inhabitants and left to go to rack and ruin.

To the left, the land fell slowly away in the direction of the highway they had just left. To the right the ground rose in barren fields enclosed in crumbling stone walls, to open moorland topped by a small hill covered in bracken and gorse. The fields themselves were a wilderness, clad alternately in rank brown grass and the bright green moss and foliage of undrained marshes. Ahead lay the silent deserted hamlet of Sprawle.

Crampitt reduced speed to a crawl to allow them to take it all in.

'Since they took Mrs. Quill to hospital this place has been deserted, except for police, newsmen and morbid sightseers. Even a few hours after the crime was discovered, you couldn't move for cars filled with people viewing the scene of the crime like a lot of vultures. In the end, we closed the road.'

They had arrived in the hamlet itself. The road passed through it and ended at a cluster of tumbledown cottages in the distance. Crampitt was still talking like a courier conducting a lot of excursionists.

'That clump of ruins at the end was once a community of crofters, who ran small farms – market gardens really – and sold their stuff on stalls at local markets. They packed up and went, one after another. They could earn better livings as roadmen, bus conductors and such like in the towns and have shops and cinemas on their doorsteps, instead of having to walk or cycle three or four miles every time they wanted a loaf or a bobbin of cotton...'

They came to the first buildings along the road, two small stone farmhouses set in narrow enclosures with old trees and bushes sadly hanging over ruined garden walls and outhouses.

'These are the two small farms I told you about. Lower Meadows and Lite's Corner.'

All the glass of the windows had been smashed by hooligans. The doors had been removed, too, and at Lower Meadows, which had a long corridor from front to back, they could see right through to the daylight beyond and the small derelict farmyard with a rotting mowing-machine in the middle of it. Half the slates of the Lite's Corner roof had been removed and the beams were bare. The small tied cottage adjoining Lite's ground had its front door nailed up. Someone had written across it *Joe loves Marlene* in paint which had once been white. The chimney had blown down and had crashed through the roof. In the overgrown front garden a torn-down, home-made sign. *Trespasers will be prosected.*

Crampitt increased speed a little and they continued their crawl along the road, which deteriorated as they progressed. Now, they bumped among the potholes and ruts and a line of grass appeared running down the middle of the broken asphalt. It was obvious that somewhere in the vicinity the Rural District Council ceased to be responsible for the road and that Quill or someone equally slovenly and parsimonious took over.

'Here we are. This is Great Lands.'

Crampitt pulled up and got out. His companions followed him, glad to limber up their limbs, stiffened in the police car too small for men of their dimensions. They all stood in front of the dilapidated farmhouse in contemplation. Crampitt leaned on the gate.

'Not much of a place, eh?'

Cromwell winked at Littlejohn behind Crampitt's back. The young detective, if such he could be called, seemed to have taken the initiative for the whole outing instead of, as instructed, simply being sent to meet them and conduct them to his superior officers. He was more like an estate agent showing them over a property and at the same time running it down because he didn't wish them to buy it.

'Must have been a nice place in its prime. Now just a tumbledown ruin.'

The farm was a massive place. Four up and four down, at least, stone built with a huge square front and broad steps ascending from a large desolate overgrown garden. In the rear they could see a series of substantial outbuildings providing a windbreak and protection for the house. The whole was surrounded by an impressive stone wall, broken by great gates in front and behind and could have been, in its heyday, completely shut off from the outside world, like those fortified Breton farmhouses strongly protected from the sea and especially from the marauders who came across it.

The front gates were open. The hinges were rusted, the wood rotten and they looked ready to collapse if you tried to move them. The beds of the front garden were covered in weeds and rank grass. At some time there must have been roses cultivated there, for there were briers, gone back to nature, rambling all over the place. Gaunt trees hung over it and the rotted leaves of past years covered the paths. A stone building, once perhaps a potting-shed, stood in one corner without a roof and from inside a tree had sprung and its trunk protruded through the spars.

'We'd better take a look over the place, just to give you some idea...'

Crampitt had brought the key with him and had unlocked the front door. They all entered.

Every house has its own peculiar smell and that of this place wasn't at all pleasant. The Quills had lived alone, the woman had been an invalid. Presumably the house had been neglected. They knew that as soon as they stepped in the hall. The kitchens, drains, damp walls and carpets, the abandonment of every effort to keep the place properly clean all contributed their share to the tainted air, shut in behind closed windows. Above all there was one dominating odour...

'Have there been some cats shut up in here?' asked Littlejohn, puffing hard at his pipe.

It seemed to remind Crampitt that he ought to counter the complaint and he took out another cheroot, handed one to Cromwell and lit them both.

'There were four cats. After Mrs. Quill and her husband's body were taken away, the cats must have been locked in. They must have hidden somewhere. We had to get the R.S.P.C.A. along to dispose of them. They were all old and helpless...'

They passed from room to room of the forlorn farmhouse. It was like a dream world, a fantastic scene from a gothic novel. Two only of the rooms seemed to have been used. The large kitchen and a small adjoining room used as a bedroom. The former was cheaply furnished with a large rough table on which the remnants of a meal, spread on old newspapers instead of a cloth, still remained. A couple of plain wooden chairs, drawn up, as their occupants had left them before the tragedy. A rocking-chair and a saddle-back upholstered in horsehair at the fireside; a large plain wooden dresser along one side, with a motley assortment of crockery arranged on the shelves.

There were no modern amenities. The kitchen was flagged and the damp stone added to the general smell of the place. Pieces of matting here and there. A stone sink with a large brass tap. The fireplace with an oven on each side was huge and blackleaded. Any hot water seemed to have been drawn from a boiler at one side. The dead remains of a small fire in the grate and two dirty pans on the hob. Great empty hooks in the beams where perhaps hams had hung in better times.

In modern days, how could such a place exist?

The rest of the house was even worse. Like a caricature of the castle of the Sleeping Beauty in which everybody has fallen asleep and dust and cobwebs had slowly obliterated all signs of normal habitation. The bedroom, with the soiled linen and a patchwork quilt jumbled on the huge, brass-knobbed double bed, just as they had been left after the crime. A chest of drawers, a cane-bottomed chair and two large cheap wardrobes, which emitted a blast of mothballs when they opened them and which contained a motley confused assortment of men's and women's clothes, moth-ridden and rotting on their hooks.

The rest of the rooms had not been used for years; some might not even have been entered. Several were bare; others contained odds and ends of furniture, all dirty, the good and the junk all indiscriminately thrown together. Now and then, they came across something unusual, something which had been beautiful, perhaps treasured once and had its period of delight.

Littlejohn felt stupefied by the mess around him and began to wonder vaguely what they were doing there at all. Crampitt was leaning against the door-frame of the kitchen, his cheroot still in the corner of his mouth, looking slightly pleased with himself, as though he were giving the other two a new type of experience, the kind they didn't encounter in their investigations in London.

'I think we've seen enough.'

Littlejohn wanted a breath of fresh air after it all.

'Let's go outside and you can tell us the facts of the case.'

Crampitt nodded and looked pleased.

'Our men have been all over the lot with a fine-tooth comb. The robbers didn't leave any traces. Nor was there anything to help with the enquiry. As I said, very little money was left. You haven't seen the dairy at the back of the kitchen. It's got a lot of old corroded equipment in it, but it hasn't been used for years. Same with the outbuildings. A lot of accumulated rubbish…'

After all, the local police were concerned with the ruins and the rubbish. Littlejohn made for the front door without more ado and stepped into the open air again. There was a fine view of the flat countryside below with the trunk roads full of traffic passing along the bottom of the slope. And Quill and his wife had retreated to their tumbledown house, shut themselves away from civilisation and allowed the rest of their world to rot and tumble about their ears.

'This is briefly how it happened...'

Crampitt was at it again.

'... Yesterday morning, a man passing on the main road from Rugby to Marcroft stopped a police car and said a farm on the hillside was on fire and he showed them the smoke billowing in the distance. It was this place, Great Lands. The alarm was given and the fire brigade and local police were soon on the spot...'

'Yes,' said Littlejohn, watching a hawk hovering over the hillside below.

'When they arrived here, they found someone had set fire to an old haystack in the farmyard...'

Cromwell looked up suddenly.

'A haystack in a farmyard!'

'Yes. If you don't believe me, take a look. It's still there, burnt out. You have to remember, this wasn't an ordinary farm. It was run by a madman. That's what I think. Quill was a madman.'

'Go on...'

Crampitt looked as if he expected an apology from Cromwell for interrupting. None came. He continued.

'It was thought that Mrs. Quill had fired it to attract attention. What else could she do? No phone, unable to walk any distance, nobody about. They found her on the doorstep, collapsed. She'd had a stroke. It took her speech and one side of her body. She's in Marcroft Hospital and she hasn't spoken a word since they found her. Until she speaks, or at least, shows any interest in what's going on, nobody will quite know what happened.'

'What about her husband?'

'I'm coming to that. They found him in the kitchen doorway, dead, with his wife beside him. He'd been killed by a blow on the back of his head. You'll see the pathologist's report at headquarters. The crime had probably been committed the night before between eight and ten o'clock. Mrs. Quill must have been left with the body for the whole night and until ten the next morning, when the fire at the farm was spotted. I suppose she was wondering how to get help. How she made her way from the house to the far side of the farmyard to fire the stack, God alone knows. She could hardly walk a yard.'

'Any traces of whoever committed the crime?'

'None whatever. Of course, that's the way the Black Lot work, isn't it?'

'You're sure it was the Black Lot.'

'Well, in view of what's been going on lately, we naturally assumed it was another of their crimes. It follows the pattern of the rest, doesn't it?'

'That remains to be seen. I suppose the results of the investigation so far will be on file at headquarters?'

'Yes. There's quite a big file, but, so far, it hasn't been of much help. Unless Mrs. Quill recovers consciousness and has something spectacular to tell us, it looks as if the Quill crime will join the rest of the Black Lot ones...'

Cromwell interrupted him.

'How long did you say you've been in the police, Sergeant Crampitt?'

'Ten years.'

'H'm.'

Crampitt didn't seem in any way affected by the hint. He led the way back to the police car.

'That be all for now?'

'For the present, yes, Crampitt,' said Littlejohn. 'We'd better report at headquarters and see what they have to say...'

When they arrived at headquarters in Marcroft, they were told that Mrs. Quill had died an hour ago without recovering consciousness.

Chapter II
A Round of Town

Although his colleagues at Marcroft were working on the assumption that the Great Lands affair was yet another of the Black Lot operations, Littlejohn had a feeling that there was more behind the death of Harry Quill than that. Furthermore, this was the first robbery they had committed at a tumbledown farm, and their first murder. In the past, they had chosen prosperous-looking but remote properties where the risk of the venture would be worth while and the trouble and care in preparing the raid would pay off.

Great Lands, in spite of its name, had no obvious attraction at all for anyone in search of easy money. Littlejohn was in Marcroft on the Farmhouse Crimes case, but this part of it seemed decidedly off-beat. Without airing his views too much to the local police, he determined to treat Quill's death as a separate case.

Superintendent Taylor, of Marcroft, seemed surprised when Littlejohn asked if there were any surviving members of the Quill family.

'Yes, sir. Quite a number. Most of them live locally. Why? Do you think they might be involved?'

'No. But I simply can't regard Quill and his wife as completely isolated, even if they were a pair of recluses. There must be others. I'd have thought several of their relatives, if they had any, would have turned up already for what they could get out of the estate or to enquire hopefully about their aunt's state of health.'

'They have. What you might call the new reigning head of the Quill lot has been here already asking for permission to go through the house and its contents in view of his aunt's infirmity and inability to help herself. We sent him packing. After all, Harry Quill's only been dead a bit more than a day. I told his nephew that we'd let him know when our investigations on the premises were finished and the house available. He went off in a huff, to see a lawyer, he said.'

'Who is this nephew?'

'Jerry Quill? He's the dead man's eldest nephew. There are several others. I don't quite know how many, but we'll find out if you like. Jerry's the county rat-catcher here in Marcroft. He describes himself as the rodent and pest officer. As far as I know, he's the only relative of Harry Quill who was welcome in or near the farm and then it wasn't for a social or family call. Sprawle hamlet, in the state it's in, is rat-ridden and Jerry used to go to his uncle's place rodent operating.'

'He lives in Marcroft?'

'Yes. I'm sorry we haven't a file on the Quill family as yet. But we'll soon attend to it, if you wish. We hadn't looked on this case from what you might call the private and personal angle. We were sure the Black Lot were involved in it, you see.'

Superintendent Taylor was a smallish man for a police officer, but what he lacked in height he made up in keenness. His pleasant round ruddy face often deceived those who didn't know him. He rarely missed a trick.

'Don't worry about a file, Superintendent. Carry on as you planned. I'll take Cromwell with me to get a picture of the Quill family background. It may prove useful.'

Taylor looked puzzled. It wasn't his business to question the methods of his superiors, but this seemed a queer red-herring. However, his staff were busy enough and if Littlejohn cared to undertake the duties usually carried out by junior officers, he was welcome to do so.

Crampitt had, much to Littlejohn's relief, been sent off on another mission. Taylor had rebuked him for taking it upon himself to show the newcomers the scene of the crime before reporting to headquarters with them. Crampitt, who had taken a university degree in economics before joining the police, thought he'd merely shown initiative which wasn't appreciated and went off confidently to exercise his talents on yet another robbery with violence, this time in the local supermarket.

A young constable called Cryer was assigned to show Littlejohn and Cromwell their hotel. It was in the Market Place. None of the surrounding hotels was of any size. This one seemed the best and had obviously been recently renovated. The entrance hall was bright with new varnish and ornamented with palms in pots. The manager seemed to know Cryer, who hadn't much to say for himself. He seemed overawed by his visitors. The manager wasn't. He ran all over the place and offered to show them the hotel from top to bottom if they wished.

'We've reserved each of you a room with a bath. We've just had new bathrooms put in. The rooms overlook the square. If there's anything you want, just say the word...'

The porter who carried up their bags didn't seem impressed with his boss.

'He's new. Turned the place upside down. He'll learn in time,' he said with relish.

Cryer left them with a stiff salute and the manager salaamed as they followed the porter. On the way up, they passed the dining-room with a lot of little tables with white cloths where a waitress was folding napkins fan-shaped and shoving them in glasses.

'We'll have a wash and then take a stroll round the place...'

The porter was waiting for his tip. Littlejohn gave him a shilling.

'Do you hold a cattle market in Marcroft?'

'*They* do. Every Monday and Wednesday. Just across the square at the back of the railway station.'

'Does it make you busy here?'

'At this hotel, do you mean? Just a bit. The better class farmers and what's left of the local gentry take lunch here, but it's not what it was. The money's in different hands these days. Most of those who go to the mart is satisfied with pies, sausage rolls and pints of beer at the pubs round the cattle pens. They wouldn't feel at home in this place, which isn't what it used to be, either. Not by a long chalk. Is there anything more?'

Littlejohn and Cromwell met in the hall ten minutes later.

'Let's take a look round the pubs near the cattle market...'

Cromwell gave Littlejohn a queer look.

'Making a good start, aren't we?'

Marcroft was a typical Midlands market town. A market square, bounded on one side by the parish church of St. Jude; on another the town hall and its offices; and the rest filled in by an assortment of banks, lawyers' offices, hotels and a good class shop or two. Every Friday and Saturday morning the square was filled to overflowing by the stalls of a vast outdoor produce market. A huge flock of pigeons seemed to dominate the place, descending to pick among the cobblestones, which the council had not yet been able to afford to replace by asphalt, and then launching themselves in a cloud and wheeling round and back again. The jackdaws of the church steeple had grown accustomed to the chimes of St. Jude's clock, but when the great bell tolled the hours, they still cast themselves into the air as though the steeple were shaking them off.

The town centre was built on a small hill and the main road through and a lot of minor side streets climbed up to it. Littlejohn and Cromwell descended one of these, a narrow traffic-free alleyway which led by a series of long steps to the lower part of the town, with the station, cattle market and a confused mass of small houses at the bottom of it.

It was not market day and the cattle pens, constructed of steel tubing, were all empty. There were a few auctioneers' sheds here and there, a weigh-house, all dominated by vast hoardings advertising on a grand scale most of the national products, food, beer and cigarettes. On one side, three public houses, almost one after another, spread themselves. *The Black Bull. The Millstone. The Drovers Inn.*

Littlejohn and Cromwell parted company and started to visit the pubs to ask the same question. Did Harry Quill ever call here when he came to the cattle market?

The landlord of the *Black Bull* gave Littlejohn a surly No right away. He recognised the police as soon as Littlejohn crossed the threshold. He was almost bankrupt and when in the trough of despond, drank his own whisky and then gave his wife a good hiding. He was only a small slip of a man, with a ferret face, but he caused the police a lot of trouble from time to time. He knew that he would probably lose his licence at the next Brewster Sessions. He showed Littlejohn the door.

'Never saw the chap in my life. If I had, I wouldn't help the police. Close the door after you.'

The Millstone had a landlady. Her husband had fallen down the stairs years ago whilst carrying the empties from a party of the Ancient Order of Drovers and Cowmen and broken his neck. She was buxom, too buxom altogether, but received Littlejohn with much more hospitality than the fellow next door. She asked him what he'd take, served him with his whisky and soda, heaved her bosom on the counter and leant on her elbows.

'Police?'

The cattle-market victuallers seemed up to all the tricks!

'Yes.'

'Harry Quill?'

'Yes.'

'I thought so. They don't have your type of detective on licensing offences. You're from Scotland Yard, aren't you? Chief Superintendent Littlejohn? Saw it in the morning paper.'

'Yes.'

'Glad to meet you. I can't tell you much. I knew him by name, that's all. He wasn't a customer here. He frequented *The Drovers*. I heard he was T.T. on religious grounds. He drank non-alcoholic cider. But he was a ladies' man. Ask Rose, the barmaid at *The Drovers*.'

'Are you sure?'

Mrs. Beecham, licensed to sell beer, wines, and spirits, according to the sign over the threshold, shook with laughter.

'You thinkin' what the ladies could see in a big fat lump like Quill. You'd be surprised. Ask Rosie. She'll tell you.'

'And that's all?'

'Isn't it enough to be going on with? Rosie has a room over the tobacconist's shop at the back of here. They used to meet there in the afternoon when *The Drovers* was closed. How a man of Quill's size managed to get up the stairs, I can't imagine. But he did...'

Mrs. Beecham didn't seem to have any more useful information and the important piece of news she had given was volunteered with spiteful relish and a smack of obscenity. Littlejohn thanked her and was glad to get away and back again in the spicy air which surrounded the cattle markets. Cromwell was nowhere to be seen. He must still be in *The Drovers*. Littlejohn found him there.

The small low-ceilinged inn was empty, except for Cromwell, when Littlejohn entered. It was the oldest licensed house in Marcroft and was due at any time to suffer extensive alterations on the orders of the licensing authorities. There was one large taproom overflowing with small marble-topped tables and a smaller alcove at one end with a heavy plain-wood table in the middle and long wooden settles all round it. The bar was in one corner, ornamented by the usual pumps and a background of bottles set on shelves with mirror backs. On the counter, a pile of meat pies on a glass stand with a large plastic cover over them. They looked like yesterday's vintage – or even the day before that.

Rosie Coggins and Cromwell were seated at one of the small tables. Cromwell had a glass of beer in front of him and Rosie a goblet with what looked like the remnants of brandy in it. Rosie's eyes were red and swollen as though she'd been having a good cry. As Littlejohn entered, Cromwell gave him a penitent sort of look, perhaps conveying that he wasn't responsible for the tears.

Cromwell introduced Rosie and Littlejohn, and Rosie burst into tears again, as though Littlejohn's compassionate look had moved her deeply. Then she wiped her eyes on the sodden handkerchief which she clutched in the palm of her hand.

'I'm sorry,' she sobbed.

She was buxom, too, but not of the proportions of her peevish rival next door. Her figure was a bit too ample, but comfortable-looking and her hair had been bleached. By her customers she was probably known as a good sort.

'I'd better get behind the bar and look as if I'm working,' she said. 'If anybody comes in and finds me in this state, they'll wonder what I've been up to.'

She looked at the clock on the wall. It was almost one o'clock.

'We close at two today. Market days, the licence is extended, but on days like this we close between two and six. I've told the gentleman most of what I could remember about Harry Quill, though. He used to come here whenever he was in the market. He's been coming for years. We were good friends. It wasn't what you think. He only took soft drinks in public, but he got to coming to my room, where he liked a bottle of stout and a talk...You must think it funny but that's all it was. He seemed a lonely sort who wanted to unburden himself of his troubles, and that's all there was to it. If you want to know any more, come back after two o'clock. We can talk here, but I can't serve you with any drinks.'

'I'd like Chief Superintendent Littlejohn to hear what you've been telling me...'

Cromwell gave Littlejohn an enquiring look. Neither of them seemed inclined to tackle the pies for lunch, so they arranged to return and went off to eat elsewhere. Rosie's company would probably have been more entertaining than that of the bustling manager of their hotel or his apparently rebellious head waiter, but there it was.

They were back at *The Drovers* at five minutes past two and Rosie let them in. Over the glass screen at the window of *The Millstone* Littlejohn saw the crafty eyes of Mrs. Beecham watching their every move.

Inside there seemed to be nobody about.

'Are you here on your own?' asked Cromwell.

'Not as a rule. But the landlord, Mr. Criggan, and his wife have gone to Rugby to see their son off. He's in the army and going out to the East. They'll be back before opening time.'

'Mind if we sit down?'

Cromwell took a seat on a tall stool at the counter and Littlejohn did the same. They were more comfortable than the chairs at the scattered tables, which were growing old and creaked as you sat on them. Rosie stood all the time.

'I'm used to being on my feet and once I sit down, my feet start to swell a bit and I don't want to get up.'

'How long have you been barmaid here?'

'Six years. I was married to one of the corporation cattle-market attendants. Everybody knew Jack. He was very popular. He was killed by a bull that went mad in the mart. Mr. Criggan gave me this job. It was good for trade because it attracted Jack's friends from among the cattle dealers and farmers… That's how I came to know Harry Quill. He was friendly with Jack through coming regular to the mart. One day, Harry Quill called here and asked for a soft drink and sort of introduced himself. After that he came often.'

'You became good friends.'

'Yes. That's all. I can't *make* you believe me, but that's all.'

There was a pause.

'Would you like some coffee? I've got some on the stove in the kitchen. It makes a change to have coffee after so much of the rest.'

She didn't wait for an answer but went off in the place behind. They could hear her opening and closing cupboard doors and rattling cups. Hardly a sound came from the market or the square outside. The clock was electric, out of keeping with the age of the place, and the whirring of its mechanism sounded above everything else.

Rose was back with three cups of coffee on a tin tray.

'Excuse the tray. We don't go in for fancy things here. Our customers aren't that type.'

She set out the cups on one of the tables and passed one each to Littlejohn and Cromwell. Then she sat down herself on one of the chairs, sipped her coffee and seemed to approve of it.

They lolled there at their ease as if they'd all been friends for years. Rosie kicked off her shoes and rubbed her feet.

'What a relief to get my shoes off. Standing about is a bit tiring...'

She didn't replace her shoes, but sat wriggling her toes voluptuously as though it gave her great pleasure.

'This isn't getting us far, is it? Did you want to know anything more about Harry Quill?'

Chapter III
The Confidences of Harry Quill

'Have you known Harry Quill long?'

'As I told you, about six years. That was just after Jack, my husband, was killed. Harry had been in the habit of calling here whenever he was in Marcroft and eating a pie and having a drink. We met on the first mart day I was here. It was months before he even said a word to me other than just to order what he wanted. Then one day he came in and I noticed that he was eating and drinking at the counter with one hand kept in his pocket. I asked him what was the matter. At first, he tried to pass it off, but I could see he was in some pain, so I persuaded him to show me his hand. The thumb was an awful sight; twice its usual size, purple and inflamed and full of pus. I told him he ought to see a doctor right away...'

She seemed a very intelligent girl and spoke nicely and politely. Circumstances which had forced her to earn her own living must have brought her down to a barmaid's job from something better in the past.

'You see, I'd been a kitchen maid in a cottage hospital before I married. There was an influenza epidemic and half the staff were off. I was sent to help in the out-patients, bringing and carrying for the doctors, and I saw quite a lot. When it was all over, they let me stay in the out-patients as a sort of orderly, as I'd done very well there and staff was hard to get. I learned things. Enough to know that Harry Quill's thumb had better not be neglected. More coffee?'

She filled up the cups and looked at the clock.

'Time's getting on and I'd better hurry. I asked Harry what he'd been doing to get such a bad hand. He said he'd had a splinter in it and had cut it out with his knife. The place was busy with men from the market and I'd no more time to discuss or persuade him. I don't know why I did it – I suppose I was sorry for him – but I told him how to find my room and said if he'd meet me there after closing time, I'd dress his hand. I'd some iodine and bandages. At first, he tried to pass it off again and I got a bit mad with him. "All right," I said. "Don't bother, then. Go home and leave it to get worse, and die." He went out without another word, but when I arrived home, he was there, standing at the door of my room, waiting. I'd seen the doctors lancing wounds and I opened his thumb with a safety-razor blade. Then I dressed it. He was a bit groggy after that, so I gave him a glass of stout...

'That needed some doing, I can tell you. The stout, I mean. He said he'd never taken alcohol before in his life. It seems his family, for generations, had belonged to a temperance society who never touched strong drink, as he called it, under any circumstances. Harry wasn't what you'd call a religious man, but he was very proud of his family and its traditions. He told me they'd been at a farm called Great Lands for generations and been much respected. You wouldn't have thought it, seeing him there in his old suit and cloth cap riding into town on his old tractor. But when you got to know him, you'd know he had his own ideas of right and wrong, mostly according to what his family had done in the past. He talked of his father as though he'd been God.'

'And you persuaded him to take to drink?'

'Well, hardly that. I told him he'd got run-down and stout would do him good. At the end, he said he'd have one glass, as medicine. After that, whenever he called here he'd drink one bottle and always say, "I'm taking my medicine," as though he was satisfying his conscience.'

'And that started his calling on you at your room?'

'Yes. Every mart day after that, he called. Of course, for weeks, his hand needed dressing. He wouldn't go to a doctor or have anybody but me do anything for it. He wore his bandage for a fortnight. It's a wonder he didn't get blood poisoning or lockjaw, because with his farming all the week, the dressing got in an awful state. In the end, it healed and he kept calling at my place every time he was in Marcroft and after he'd eaten his pie and drunk his sarsaparilla, as the drovers called it when they tried to pull his leg.'

'And this continued right until he died?'

Her lip quivered. She sat with her chin in her hands and her elbows on the table. She never took her eyes off Littlejohn.

'Yes. It seemed as if we'd known each other always, in the end. At first, he didn't talk much. Then, he broke the ice. He seemed to want somebody to confide in ...'

Littlejohn could quite see it. Rosie was a sympathetic, comfortable sort. She just talked and asked no questions. Not the inquisitive or possessive type. She was clean and attractive, and self-possessed enough to deal with any customers who tried to take liberties.

'And anybody who says there was anything more between us than just friendship, is a liar...'

She flared up, as though they might be doubting the relationship.

'He used to stay till I'd to go back for opening time. Then we shook hands and he went.'

Littlejohn could well imagine that Quill had to make an effort of will to get up and take himself off after he'd opened his heart, drunk his bottle of stout and enjoyed the sympathy of Rosie. She seemed to have been his only friend, his only real contact with humanity.

'What did you talk about when he called on you?'

She gave him an astonished look.

'That's rather a tall order, isn't it? We met once or twice a week for an hour or so for more than five years! You can't expect me to tell you all that went on. I can't even remember myself.'

'Did he tell you about his past?'

'Now and then. I never pressed or questioned him about it. We sort of just took one another for granted. If he'd anything on his mind when he called, he told me about it. He didn't seem to be one who worried much. He was what some would call a queer sort. With his red face and old clothes, you might have taken him for a hill-billy farmer, but he wasn't. He'd been educated at Marcroft Grammar School when he was a boy. He told me that once when I asked him how he came to speak so nicely and use just the right word. His father had insisted on his boys having a proper education.'

'Did Mr. Quill talk a lot about his family?'

'Yes, a lot. He was proud of his family. I never knew what his farm was like; I didn't take the liberty of spying on him or prying into his affairs. But he once told me that his farm was called Great Lands and was at Sprawle and that when he was a boy, it had been a very big one with servants and farm-hands about the place and how they came to Marcroft on market days in a pony-trap. They must have been rich. In fact, Harry might still have been rich. I never asked him. He offered to pay for what he called my attentions, when I'd looked after his infected hand. I lost my temper a bit and told him never to offer me money again. He never did. At Christmas and my birthday, he'd bring along a big box of chocolates or a large iced cake with my name on it. That was all I'd ever take from him. I enjoyed his company and I said so. My father was a chemist; owned his own shop. He went bankrupt and committed suicide and it killed my mother. I was educated at a convent school and at fourteen found myself in an orphanage. I ran away. Harry Quill and I both seemed to have come down in the world. Harry said the farm wasn't what it was. He'd had bad luck with it. That's perhaps what attracted us to one another.'

The clock on the wall whirred away the time and still they hadn't got anywhere. It was quiet and comfortable in the old pub and with no business going on in the cattle market, the square was peaceful and deserted. Littlejohn seemed to have captured the mood of Quill, sitting there, talking about nothing much, just waiting until opening-time when Rosie would have to get about her business again.

'Did Harry Quill ever mention what had put an end to the prosperity of Great Lands?'

'Not exactly. But I do remember one day when he came to see me, he was late and said he'd been at a solicitor's office...'

'He had a lawyer then. Do you know his name?'

'I remembered it. Harry complained that his fees were high. It was Mr. Nunn. His office is in the Market Square up in the town.'

Littlejohn nodded to Cromwell who made a note of it in his big black notebook.

'Go on, Mrs. Coggins. You were telling us about the decline of Great Lands.'

'Call me Rosie. It sounds less official. He'd been at the solicitor's office and he said that he'd bought back the last of the old place. He said it as if he was quite proud of it. I didn't ask about it. I never tried to pry in his private affairs, but he told me. It seems his father had inherited the farm from *his* father and it was a fine one of more than five hundred acres. Then, he'd started speculating and lost money. He'd sold off a hundred acres to somebody who'd got a cottage near Great Lands and the man who bought the land made another small farm of it. That wasn't enough to pay the debts, however, and he sold another hundred to a buyer who made another small farm by rebuilding another old cottage nearby. It broke his father's heart, he said, because he loved his land. He actually left instructions that soil from the farm had to be laid under his coffin when he was buried. Harry said he swore when he inherited the three hundred acres from his father that, come what may, he'd get back the land his father had sold and restore Great Lands to its former prosperity. He bought the land when he got the chance and ended with the five hundred acres again.'

'Have you seen Great Lands recently?'

'No. As I told you, I never went there. I was afraid I might meet Harry and he'd be annoyed at me spying on him. Why?'

'It is a wilderness. He got back his lost acres, but he either hadn't the money to develop them or else something occurred which made him lose all interest in farming. Much of the land has gone back to the wild now. The place, house and land, is desolate.'

Her mouth opened slightly and her eyes widened.

'I don't understand...'

'How long ago was it that he bought the last of the land his father had sold?'

'I'd say two years ago, at a guess.'

'And after that, did he change in any way? Did he seem to have lost interest or to deteriorate?'

'No. Not that I'd know.'

'Did he ever seem short of money?'

'No. He always had plenty of money in cash in his pockets. You see, he'd call here after he'd been in the mart and sold whatever he had brought in with him or sent down in the cattle van that picked up the livestock from the farms around.'

'What did he sell?'

'Cattle and sheep. He told me he reared cattle for beef...'

'There was no stock on the farm when he died. Could he have sold out when he lost interest?'

'He might have done. Just for something to say when he arrived, I'd ask if he'd had a good morning in the mart. He'd either shrug his shoulders or else pass it off with a laugh.'

'So, it might be that eventually, he simply came to town to see you, not to visit the mart?'

'If he did, he never hinted at it.'

'He was secretive about some things?'

'Yes.'

'About his wife, for example?'

'Not exactly. He told me about her. She was an invalid. He said she was his cousin and had lived at Great Lands with his father and mother, helping in the house, when they were alive. He'd always liked her and they'd married when the old people had turned over the farm to Harry. There had been one child, but something went wrong at his birth and he died and Mrs. Quill nearly died as well. Soon after that, she got polio and lost the use of one side; her arm and leg were paralysed. That's all I know, except that Harry had a lot to do for her and I know from what he said that he treated her well and thought well of her.'

'But that tragedy all happened long before Harry met you and bought back the land his father had lost?'

'Oh, yes. Years before.'

'So it can't be that he lost heart because he'd never have a son to leave Great Lands to when he died.'

'No, never. He never hinted at such a thing. He was loyal to Mrs. Quill. As I said, he never made a pass at me. He wasn't that sort. In his young days he might have had a good time. I don't know. He never talked about his past in that way. He was turned fifty when I got to know him. He was a man who, somehow, didn't seem to want to be involved. He never made friends with any of the other farmers or dealers in the mart. He just did his business, ate his snack at the bar here, and then came for a talk with me and went back home. I'm surprised he had time for me, but he had. Even then, he was reserved. The furthest he ever went with me was to say if ever I needed a friend, to think of him first and he'd see me through any trouble I had, money or anything else.'

'Did you ever need his help?'

'No. I'm an independent sort. I managed.'

'You must have had your admirers. Did Harry Quill resent that? Was he a jealous sort?'

She took it quite as a matter of course. She didn't even blush or preen herself.

'In a job like mine, I have my ups and downs. Some of the men who come here are the rough sort. They get fresh sometimes. But I know how to take care of myself. I didn't need any help from Harry on that score. He never had any cause for complaint.'

'Harry Quill was murdered...'

'I saw it in the paper. I've not known whether I was on my head or my heels since. Do you think they'll catch the men who did it? I read about them in the paper, too. I just can't believe it. To choose Harry Quill of all people and to kill him like that...'

Tears began to run down her cheeks, but she created no fuss. Littlejohn waited.

'Do you know of anyone who might have held a grudge against Harry Quill? Who might want to murder him?'

She gave him a blank look.

'I thought you knew who'd done it!'

'We can't be sure.'

'I thought you might call. I'm glad you came. Whoever it was killed Harry was a swine. Harry wouldn't harm anybody. He was a good sort. You don't meet many of his kind nowadays.'

'Mrs. Quill has just died, too.'

'They surely didn't...'

'No. She was alone with her husband when it happened and had no way of summoning help. She had to set fire to a haystack to attract attention and the effort was too much. She had a stroke and died after it.'

'How awful! I'm glad you came, but I can't help you much. I'll do all I can. I've nothing to hide. I'm glad it's you, though, and not the local police. They might have made trouble for me.'

'Why?'

'This place hasn't too good a reputation. None of the public houses round the market have. A lot of the market men come here and drink a lot. They get unruly now and then and Mr. Criggan has to call in the police sometimes. They might have misunderstood my relations with Harry... You know what I mean.'

It was four o'clock. The time seemed to have slipped quickly away and still they were no nearer.

'Mr. and Mrs. Criggan will be back any time...'

'And you wouldn't like them to find us here?'

'It might lead to complications. They're all right, but they'll naturally jump to conclusions if they find me with the police. They knew about Harry and me being friends. Who doesn't, in these parts? They've hinted that we were more than friends and tried to pull my leg about it. I had a row with them and told them I'd leave if there was any more of it and they've been quiet about it since. I do most of the work here and they'll not get another to do as much. They know it. But if they found the police here... Well, it's only natural, isn't it? They wouldn't want to be mixed up in a murder case, would they?'

'We'll go then. But we may need you again. In that case, we'd better call on you in your lodgings when this place is closed. We'll let you know.'

'I'm usually at home about three o'clock in the afternoon, except on Mondays and Wednesdays, when the licensing hours are extended. I'm home at four, those days.'

'One other question before we go, Rosie. Had Harry Quill any relatives?'

'He'd had one other brother, who died some years ago. That brother had three sons, Jerry, Herbert and Tim. Jerry's the oldest. He's the corporation rat-catcher in Marcroft. Herbert lives just outside Marcroft on the south side and works for the water-board. Tim's in Branscombe, ten miles away. He's a farmer there and seems to have done pretty well for himself. I know all about the Quill family, you see. Harry was always talking about his family. Pity he never had any children of his own.'

'Which was his favourite nephew?'

'Tim. He liked Tim best because he'd stuck to farming. Harry was fond of the land. He hadn't much patience with Jerry and Herbert, who'd started in farming, but chose what Harry called soft town jobs. Jerry was the one who saw the most of his uncle. I suppose, as the eldest, he fancied he'd come into the property if anything happened to Harry. Tim was more independent. He never visited his aunt and uncle. The only contact they had was when Tim's wife sent them a card at Christmas.'

'And those were all?'

'There were cousins, but they weren't close. Harry never encouraged the family to visit Great Lands. He said they were a poor lot and Tim was the only real Quill among them.'

'You never met any of them?'

'No. Why should I? I know Jerry by sight. He comes to the mart hunting for vermin, doing his job, but I only see him in the distance. He knew his uncle didn't welcome his visits to the farm, so called on the excuse that he'd to inspect the place for rats. I doubt whether he was ever allowed indoors.'

'Thank you, Rosie. We'll see you later, then.'

Littlejohn knew she'd have a good cry after they'd gone.

Back at Marcroft police station Superintendent Taylor was in a decidedly peevish mood.

'I've some news for you, Chief Superintendent. I didn't know where to find you. It's important. Alters the whole aspect of the case.'

He tried to keep them on tenterhooks by rummaging among the files on his desk. Finally he unearthed a slip of paper on which were written some cryptic notes.

'The Black Lot were all arrested near Elrick, Aberdeen, on the night Harry Quill was killed. So they couldn't have murdered Quill.'

He paused for effect.

'There's no doubt whatever that it was the Black Lot?'

'No doubt at all, sir. There were three of them and they answered to the descriptions circulated. They'd followed their usual routine of committing a crime at the other end of the earth from where they'd last appeared. The farm was remote and occupied by the owner and his wife, who were reputed to be well-off. But this time the black boys had missed something when they cased the place. The farmer, a man called Cullen, had two police dogs lodging with him. It seems he breeds Alsatians and has a nephew in the force in Aberdeen. The dogs had been a bit off colour and were due for a rest, so Cullen's nephew took them to the farm for a few days and left them there on the very afternoon of the crime. When the Black Lot arrived, Cullen had the dogs with him in the kitchen and set them on the robbers, one of whom tried to shoot a dog and wished he hadn't. The dogs dealt with one apiece and Cullen, who's wrestled in the highland games, settled the other. A sorry set of circumstances for the Black Lot. They'll have quite a spectacular trial when their time comes.'

'Was Cullen on the phone?'

'Yes; they cut the wires. It's a wild spot and ideal for the gang, but, as the wires are often down in winter, Cullen had a second string in case of emergency. Two coastguard rockets. After he'd strung up the intruders he gave a firework display that brought up the local police from the valley. So that's the end of their career for a bit.'

Taylor paused for breath.

'That puts a different aspect on Harry Quill's murder, doesn't it? We'll have to start all over again on a new tack.'

He sat back in his chair and waited for the reaction.

'We've already done that, Superintendent.'

'Eh?'

'We've made a start by interviewing a lady friend of Harry Quill.'

'You don't let the grass grow under your feet, do you? Who is she?'

Littlejohn told him of their visit to Rosie Coggins and the information she'd volunteered.

'That's a start anyway. Are you going to turn it over to us now or...?'

'Could you do with a little help?'

Littlejohn was thinking of Rosie and her fear of the local police. After all, he and Cromwell had established friendly relations which might be turned to good purpose.

'I certainly could do with some help if you can spare the time.'

All Taylor's annoyance had vanished. Murders were rare in his parish and assistance from a couple of experts wouldn't come amiss.

'As the Black Lot are out of our hair, we might arrange it. This is a pleasant part of the world and a little rural work might come as a change after London.'

'Right. It's all yours.'

Littlejohn filled his pipe and lit it.

'Officially, this is a corollary of the Black Lot investigation. I'm sure someone who killed Quill hoped those boys would be saddled with the crime. We'll give him a surprise.'

Chapter IV
Legal Opinion

From the police station they made a round of telephone calls to the banks in the town. Did a farmer called Harry Quill... or was it Henry?... keep an account with them? One had an account in the name of Timothy Quill; another Herbert; and a third, Gerald. But nobody claimed the business of Harry. They tried the building society offices, too, and drew a blank.

'Perhaps Harry's lawyer, Mr. Nunn, will know where he kept his money,' said Littlejohn. 'Where's his place?'

Taylor showed him from the window of his office.

'Just across the square in the new office block there... How did you find that out?'

'From Rosie.'

Somehow, Littlejohn couldn't help calling Quill and Rosie by their Christian names. He might have known them all his life.

'So, she was smart enough to find out all about Quill's business affairs.'

'On the contrary. She discovered it quite by accident. I'll just walk across and see Mr. Nunn and Cromwell might try to find the rat-catcher. What's his name...? Jerry... And see what sort of chap he is and how much he knows.'

Cromwell bared his teeth in a mirthless grin.

'I hope he's not down the sewers.'

Taylor didn't think it funny.

'Jerry dresses up like an official and you won't find him digging for rats. He's got an assistant who does the dirty work.'

'What's the name of Nunn's firm?'

'Nunn, Spencer and Nunn. You'd better ask for Mr. Leslie Nunn. He's the family lawyer; Spencer does the court work.'

Mr. Nunn was in and saw Littlejohn right away. He was a tall, thin man, with a lined clean-shaven face. He was a bit nondescript and Littlejohn found it difficult to guess his age.

The premises occupied by the firm were new and many-storeyed and had replaced an ancient building which had contained a rabbit warren of offices and small warehouses. The lawyers' suite was the best of the lot and on the ground floor. Most of the furniture was of steel, but Mr. Leslie Nunn had made an exception in his own case and set himself up in an atmosphere of antiques. The room was large, there were one or two good water colours on the walls between cases of law books and reports, and Mr. Nunn was seated at an appropriately large old mahogany desk which must have cost him a pretty penny. He looked tired.

'Take a seat, Chief Superintendent…'

He spoke slowly and deliberately. In spite of his languor he was a tidy and careful man. Neat in his dress and neat in his speech.

He pressed a button on a contraption on his desk and spoke into it.

'Bring in the sherry, please.'

He might, judging by the way he said it, have been ordering several barrels of it. A girl arrived with a decanter and glasses, which looked like collector's pieces and placed them on the desk.

'You'll join me?'

Littlejohn said he would, thank you. The drink was in keeping with the occasion, astringent, with the tightness of alum in the mouth.

Mr. Nunn sighed again, this time with approval of his drink.

'You are here on the black gang case, Chief Superintendent?'

'Yes, sir, but we've just learned that Quill was murdered by someone else. The gang were operating elsewhere at the time and were captured there. So that means starting all over again on Quill's investigation. I believe you were his lawyer, Mr. Nunn?'

Mr. Nunn took a cigarette from a gold case and offered one to Littlejohn.

'I'd prefer my pipe, sir.'

'By all means...Before I answer your question, do you mind saying who informed you that Quill was a client of ours? He was a secretive man who almost sneaked in our office when he came. That was during our occupation of the old premises...'

'A friend of his, Rose Coggins, barmaid at the *Drovers Inn.*'

'Ah; his mistress, eh?'

'She'd be very annoyed if you told her that. She swears their relations were perfectly innocent.'

'I'm glad you told me. It might save some embarrassment later. I shall have to see Mrs. Coggins in a short time. She's Quill's sole residuary legatee.'

If Littlejohn was surprised at the news, Mr. Nunn seemed quite unmoved about it. He sighed again and passed his hand over his thin, carefully brushed fair hair.

'I'm telling you that in the strictest confidence and rather hypothetically. We made a will for him about two years ago. The farm and all the rest of his estate was left in trust for his wife and on her death, the whole passes to Mrs. Coggins. I understand that Mrs. Quill died yesterday. So, now Mrs. Coggins inherits the lot. But...'

The lawyer paused for effect.

'But... After he'd signed the will, Quill took it away with him. We have an unsigned copy here, but I couldn't persuade him to leave the original in our possession. He may have torn it up or made another for anything I know. If it still exists, there's likely to be a family row about it, isn't there?'

The idea of further litigation seemed to please Mr. Nunn. He re-filled Littlejohn's sherry glass and his own and the very taste of his drink seemed to delight him. He crossed his legs and expanded.

'We've been lawyers of the Quill family for generations. The deeds of their Great Lands go back to the time of the great enclosures. They were once common land, filched by a lord of the manor and sold. Quills have owned them ever since. Now, they might be about to pass from the family into the hands of a barmaid.'

Nunn gave Littlejohn a thin careworn smile as though the whole affair were a distasteful nuisance.

'It's hardly likely that the Quill family are going to give way without a tussle.'

'From what I hear, Harry Quill's father almost lost his farm years ago.'

'You seem very well informed. You're right, of course. Ben Quill was bitten by the bug of stock exchange speculation and came a bad cropper. It took all his cash and some sales of his land to put him straight. We dealt with the affair for him. My father was then alive and handled it. Then, when Harry inherited Great Lands, he became obsessed with the idea of restoring the lost fields to the family farm. He succeeded, but beggared himself in the process. He said it was his father's dying wish that the land be restored and he would honour it. But he hadn't any capital left to work the place. It had grown so dilapidated that nobody would grant a mortgage on it. We tried to find someone for him, but weren't successful. Mrs. Quill had money of her own, but he couldn't persuade her to part with a penny. I don't blame her. That was all they had to live on and I assume that has kept them alive whilst the farm tumbled in ruins about their heads.'

'Where was Mrs. Quill's money? We've searched the house in the course of our investigations, but there are no papers there. No wills, not even cash, except small change.'

'We have all Mrs. Quill's investments here, *and* her will, which, in confidence again, leaves all she has to her niece, Evelyn Bradley, née Quill.'

'That explains some of Harry Quill's peculiarities during recent years. Having pursued his fixed idea of restoring the farm to its original acreage, he found himself penniless and unable to work it. So, he went to seed.'

'Exactly.'

'But he must have known when he bought back the land that he hadn't any funds to work it with and would simply have to watch the whole farm deteriorate.'

'He knew that *he* hadn't the funds, but was depending on his wife putting in her money. Remember, she, too, was a Quill and infected with the family love of the land at Great Lands. But...'

Another dramatic pause.

'But, before Harry bought the last of the land which took all he had, she'd discovered the existence of Rosie Coggins. She thought the worst of that and closed the door on him as far as help with her money was concerned. I never blamed her. If she hadn't put her foot down they'd both have starved.'

'How did Mrs. Quill get to know about Rosie, I wonder.'

That was no problem for Mr. Nunn.

'Whether Rose Coggins was Quill's mistress or just his bosom friend, he behaved in a stupidly furtive manner about her and thus led people to think the worst. Most of the men in the market knew about his visits to the rooms above the tobacco shop in Eastchurch Street. I hear he used to enter the place looking like a schoolboy and glancing behind and over his shoulder to make sure he wasn't observed. Some people seem to have a nose for illicit goings-on. Whoever started the ball rolling, the tale soon got round the market. Which means that the Quill nephews would quickly hear about it. You can be sure one of them...my bet's on Jerry...would be off hot-foot to break the news to auntie. As they didn't know what I knew about the will, those boys had expectations when Uncle Harry died. They didn't want all the inheritance they imagined waiting for them, squandered on a barmaid like Rosie. It must have been a nightmare to Jerry and Herbert. Tim is a bit more sensible and he's wealthy and probably didn't care a hang...'

'You knew Mrs. Quill very well?'

'Of course. There aren't many Quills our firm haven't done business with at one time or another. Even the irreproachable Tim once called for our help on a drunken driving charge arising from too much champagne at a party. Most of the Quills are teetotallers and Tim, now moving in a circle prone to cocktail parties, has renounced the family habit. Gerald, of course, is almost an alcoholic...'

'Mrs. Quill, sir. What kind of woman was she?'

'I believe that when she was young and before illness struck her, she was a very bonny girl. She was the daughter of Quill's Uncle Luke and thus Harry Quill's cousin. A lot of people assumed that Harry married her to keep the money in the family. That's quite a habit in the rural parts of this neighbourhood. But there was more to it than that. My late father, who all his working life dealt with the legal work for the Quill family, told me what happened. The old story. Millie, Harry's wife, was left an orphan when in her 'teens and Harry's father, Ben, took her on at the farm as a sort of dairymaid and general help. Harry seduced her and had to marry her. The child died soon after birth and, I believe, Millie herself almost did the same when it was born. Her mother, who died a couple of years after her father, left Millie a few thousands which, as time went on, increased in size. It was well invested when she got it and she left it where it was and it appreciated. The certificates were lodged with us and still remain here. All Harry Quill's efforts must have failed to persuade Millie to touch her nest-egg. They lived on the income after Harry had spent all he had on his fantastic scheme of recovering the family lands.'

'If Mrs. Quill was an invalid, how did she make her will and deal with other matters requiring a lawyer?'

'A member of our staff went to see her at the farm. She always chose a time when her husband was in Marcroft on one of his periodic visits, so he was never present to interfere or know what was going on.'

'You yourself didn't go?'

'No.'

Littlejohn was sure he didn't! Mr. Nunn in his impeccable black jacket, striped trousers, with not a hair out of place, and a monocle on a black cord stuck in one of his waistcoat pockets, would have been quite out of place among the muck and debris of Great Lands.

'No. Our Mr. Bilbow always went to see her. They got on very well together.'

Mr. Nunn spoke into his desk telephone.

'Mr. Bilbow; kindly come in.'

There was a pause. Mr. Bilbow seemed to be preparing himself to enter the holy of holies. Finally he arrived.

A small man, shabbily dressed, with his features almost hidden in a short Vandyke beard. He was probably in his middle forties. He had a flushed Roman nose, which, to those who knew his history, betrayed the secret of his downfall. He had been a brilliant lawyer – still was, when he set his mind to it – but his uncertain habits had reduced him from a partnership in a good London firm to a legal hack in Nunn's office. Nevertheless, he was almost indispensable to Nunns, for he was not only a formidable legal draughtsman, but ingenious in preparing briefs. He entered with the appearance and aroma of a dedicated whisky drinker.

Nunn introduced them. Bilbow was well-spoken and good mannered and quite sober. He agreed that he and Mrs. Quill had always hit it off well.

'She was a reasonable woman and very shrewd. She protected her money like a tigress her young. The dividends on her investments were remitted to our firm and once a quarter, I called on her and handed over the accrued amount in cash. She then put it in a cash box which she kept in a locked drawer of a little desk she had in her bedroom.'

'It wasn't there when we searched the place.'

Bilbow shrugged his shoulders at Littlejohn's comment.

'Did you expect to find it? I hear that it was a case of robbery with violence.'

'Quite right. I suppose the pair of them used the cash to live on.'

'Yes. She told me so. A strange woman. From all descriptions of the life the pair of them led, you'd imagine her as a sort of mute recluse, but when I was there, she was nothing of the kind. She talked a lot, as though, after being imprisoned by her illness for so long, she craved for news of the world outside. She asked about everybody and everything.'

'Anyone or anything in particular?'

'"Any news, Mr. Bilbow, since last we met?" she'd say, and I'd rack my brains and tell her odds and ends I thought would interest her. She asked questions. Mainly about her old friends – most of whom were dead – and about their nephews, Tim, Jerry and Herbert. Evelyn, her niece, was her favourite and often called on her when Harry was in town. Living as she did, Mrs. Quill wasn't at all ignorant of what was going on outside.'

'Now, this is important, Mr. Bilbow; how mobile was Mrs. Quill? Could she get around the house or even outside?'

'No, sir. One arm and one leg were completely out of commission. I'd imagine she could have moved short distances by struggling from her chair and then hopping along, but I never saw her do it. She was always in her chair in the kitchen when I called. I once asked her if she'd never tried a wheel-chair. She said the inside of the house was too cluttered up with furniture to navigate properly and the outside was too rough and rocky and she'd overturn. I'd imagine she could perhaps have manoeuvred herself here and there in the house when she was alone. But I know Harry Quill did a lot for her. She once told me he did most of the housework and got the meals ready. Judging from the state of the place, Harry wasn't very adept at domestic science. It was like a slum.'

'Yes; when Mrs. Quill was found after she'd raised the alarm by firing a haystack, she was on the back doorstep in the farmyard. Quite a distance for one so immobile.'

Bilbow shook his head.

'She must have crawled then. She couldn't possibly have walked or even hopped there.'

'Her husband's body was found just outside the door of the farmhouse. As you know, we thought, as first, that it was another escapade of the gang known as the Black Lot...'

Mr. Nunn, who had been leaving Littlejohn undisturbed to interview Bilbow and showing his lack of concern by perusing some papers on his desk with a monocle screwed in one eye, suddenly raised his eyebrows and the monocle dropped to the end of its cord.

'Do you think it might be a family affair?'

'I've no idea, sir. We're starting all over again.'

Bilbow's teeth showed through his beard.

'You aren't, by any chance, thinking Mrs. Quill murdered Harry, are you?'

'It had never entered my head.'

'Because she certainly didn't. I've visited her professionally quite a lot, unknown to her husband, of course, and had a chance to study her and get to know her. Had she even been face to face with him, she positively wouldn't have been able to strike him down. It's ridiculous!'

Mr. Nunn's eyes opened wide again.

'No need to be so damned vehement about it, Bilbow. You ought to be well aware the police have to think of every eventuality.'

'She was a very decent old girl.'

'Hot tempered?'

'Not a bit of it. Querulous at times, but who wouldn't be, incapacitated as she was? She was a very gallant woman, who never complained about her condition or even Harry's goings-on when he came to town. She was mentally very efficient and well able to look after her affairs.'

'Did she ever ask you about Quill's relations with Rose Coggins?'

Bilbow paused and coughed.

'I promised I wouldn't mention that to a soul, but now she's dead, I guess it doesn't matter. Yes, she did. She said she'd heard, I suppose from one of her relatives, that Harry had a girl-friend in town. I said I wouldn't know. "Find out, then," she said. I made discreet enquiries.'

'With what result?'

'I made some oblique investigations in the cattle mart and pubs around...'

A congenial task!

'... It was quite well known that something was going on between Harry and Rosie, the barmaid at the *Drovers Inn*. She had a room over a tobacco shop in the alley behind the mart and Quill had been seen furtively entering the separate door to the upstairs premises. I went and had a drink at the *Drovers*. Rosie was in attendance. I thought Harry had good taste. She seemed a nice, civil decent girl. How or why she took up with Harry I wouldn't know.'

'I've met Rosie. I agree with you. She swore there was nothing but friendship between her and Harry Quill.'

Mr. Nunn made a puffing noise of contempt, but Bilbow didn't.

'She may be telling the truth. Perhaps Harry was just wanting somebody to be a mother to him. Rosie would fill the bill.'

Littlejohn lit his pipe.

'It doesn't matter, does it? Mother or mistress, she's genuinely upset by his death and I don't think her interest in him was a commercial one. However, I take it you reported to Mrs. Quill, Mr. Bilbow.'

'Yes, I did, next time I went to Great Lands.'

'How did Mrs. Quill take it?'

'Calmly. Very calmly. She thought for a bit, but she wasn't in the least excited...'

He paused.

Next door someone was typing furiously, thudding the carriage of the machine at the end of each line. The little bell on the carriage kept ringing before every thud. It seemed to get on Mr. Nunn's nerves, for he winced as the racket interrupted Bilbow's narrative, which, now and then, seemed to get lost in his beard.

'... "I'm not surprised," she finally said. "But you'd better alter my will right away. I wish to leave all my estate to my niece, Evelyn, instead of, as now, to my husband. See to it." I did as she asked and she signed a new will.'

'How long ago would that be?'

Bilbow thought for a minute.

'I'd say four years ago.'

'You seem to know quite a lot about the Quill family, Mr. Bilbow. Would any of them wish to kill Harry Quill?'

Bilbow seemed a bit taken aback by the direct question.

'Why should they? Had it been Mrs. Quill, you might have said she was vulnerable on account of her small property, but she died a natural death, really. But Harry... They all knew that he hadn't a bean. Everybody knew that. And what the Quill family don't know about one another isn't worth knowing. They knew that all Harry possessed was his tumbledown farm and its wasted acres. Who'd want to inherit that? It would need a fortune to put it to rights. Have you seen it? Hardly a field that isn't or hasn't gone to the wild. Ditches and drainage all to pot, a lot of it marshland, acres overgrown with couch grass and weeds... Who'd want to kill anybody to acquire a rubbish dump like Great Lands has become...?'

Mr. Nunn seemed utterly bored with the whole business and began to pace up and down the room, pausing at the window now and then to watch the workmen in the square setting up the stalls for the next day's produce market and gazing blankly at the traffic lights busily changing from reds to greens and back again...

Bilbow looked impatient, too. It was probably his time for slipping out to the pub behind the premises for his frequent stimulant.

It was no use prolonging the interview.

'Thank you both. That will be all.'

Mr. Nunn seemed taken aback.

'Nothing more?'

Perhaps he expected some disclosures from Littlejohn now.

'Nothing more for the time being.'

Bilbow excused himself and left rather hurriedly. Mr. Nunn still seemed uneasy, as though he'd something more to say. But Littlejohn decided he'd had enough for the present, shook the proffered hand and left Nunn to his pacing.

Chapter V
The Rat Race

When Gerald Arthur Quill was given a small office next door to the mortuary in the Town's Yard at Marcroft, Parkinson's Law began at once to operate and, as there was accommodation for three persons, at a pinch, in the room, he soon gathered to himself a couple of assistants. Jerry himself was described on the door of the place: *G. A. Quill, Rodent Officer*. His staff consisted of Jacques, an old man as skilled in rat-catching as the Pied Piper, who did all the dirty work whilst Jerry entered details about it in the records, and Douglas, a backward lad who carried the tools, cans of poison and other lethal equipment of the department whenever they were called out to a case.

When Cromwell arrived to see Jerry, he found him in a very disturbed state, for his Uncle Harry's body was lying in the morgue next door. This fact was publicly manifest by the fact that the corporation's disused steam-roller was standing in the open air in the yard. Normally, this museum piece occupied the mortuary shed, but it had to be removed whenever there was a corpse on hand. The pathologist, too, carried out his investigations there, pending the erection of a fine new laboratory elsewhere, which had, however, been postponed owing to national and local economic crises.

Jerry gave Cromwell an ungracious reception.

'I wish you police would get on with the job instead of concocting theories that don't come off.'

'I'm sorry, Mr. Quill. We're doing our best...'

'I don't know what your worst is like, then. How would you like to have your murdered uncle's body in the next room to you all the time? It's distractin'. I can't concentrate on me work.'

'But the inquest has been held and the coroner's issued a certificate of burial.'

'But there's nowhere to put him till the funeral. They can't send him back home to Great Lands. There's nobody there. And none of his relatives want him with them under the circumstances...'

Jerry Quill was a tall, heavy shambling sort of man with peppery-coloured hair and a peppery moustache. His eyelids were naturally red rimmed but he looked to have been weeping a lot. His nose was large and misshapen, as though at some time he'd had it broken and it had been badly set. He wore a dark suit, a sky-blue shirt and a red tie, and brown shoes with thick rubber soles. He never went down among the rats, but held, he maintained, an advisory post. He dressed in what he thought was administrative style, but sartorially he looked a mess.

'I called to ask you a few questions about your late uncle. I gather you were the only member of the family who regularly visited him.'

'That is so, if you can call being kept at the door in all sorts of weather visitin'. But you needn't waste your time on me. I'm a busy man and haven't any to waste on you. I know nothin' about my uncle that others can't tell you. I suppose you found that he was keepin' another woman. You'd better go and ask her. He thought more of her than his family...'

'We've already done so.'

For the first time, Jerry showed interest. His cloudy eyes narrowed.

'What did she tell you?'

'She assured us that there was nothing but friendship between her and your uncle.'

'You're surely not goin' to be taken in by a tale like that, are you? It's as plain as the nose on your face they were carryin' on together. At his age, too. He ought to have known better. She was after his money, that's what it amounted to.'

'Nobody has any proof that it was other than Rose Coggins says.'

Jerry brushed it aside.

'A barmaid! He might have chosen somebody better class than that.'

Cromwell briefly pictured Jerry and his uncle together; the nephew in his bright blue shirt and brown shoes and Harry without a collar and with a brass stud shining in the neckband of his shirt. High class! Then he remembered that the Quills were a family who considered themselves a cut above most folk, however they dressed and whatever they did.

Jerry seemed to be thinking the same.

'There have been Quills in these parts for more than three hundred years. Great Lands was a sort of manor 'ouse before Uncle Harry and his dad ruined it with their excesses. Quills was a proud family in those days.'

'Rose Coggins seemed a decent sort when we interviewed her.'

'What do you know of her? You've only been here a day and met her once. Don't jump to conclusions. My Uncle Harry was seen regular sneakin' up to her room. What else was he goin' there for but…but…immoral purposes? The old rake!'

Cromwell got nettled.

'Oh, dry up! What does it matter what he went to see her for? They were friends, whatever else they were. This is a murder case, not an enquiry into the victim's morals. As I said, you seem to have been the only member of the family who visited the farm recently. What did your uncle do when he was at home? Was he occupied with farming or just loafing about watching the place tumble about his ears?'

Jerry had started to sulk after Cromwell's sharp words, but now he shed his grievances and started to lament again.

'He was usually indoors indulging in his favourite occupation of sittin' in a rockin' chair, rockin' and smokin' his pipe. I never knew anybody so taken with a rockin' chair. It's a wonder he didn't wear the floor away. You see, he'd spent all his ready cash on buyin' back the land his father sold to pay his debts. Said he'd made old Ben a promise on his dyin' bed. He'd nothin' left to run the damn place with. My aunt had some money of her own, but she wouldn't let him have it. So, with no stock and his farming implements just a lot of old scrap iron, there was nothin' he could do. She provided the bread and butter, so to speak, and that was all. Now and then, when the buildings of the house got so bad that the rain poured in, my uncle would go and strip slates and such like from the roofs of the empty cottages on his land and repair his own. There's a chapel on the land. The Quills built it more than a century ago, but as everybody left the hamlet, it fell into disuse. Uncle Harry finally stripped and sold all the pews and panelling, even the Communion table. Then he started to take slates and wood off the roof. I told him no good would come of it, robbin' a church, and I was right.'

Jerry tried to look affronted by such impiety, but without much success.

'Did your brothers never go to visit their uncle?'

'They haven't been for a long time. It's no joke making your way to a god-forsaken spot like Sprawle and then being chased off. That's what Uncle Harry used to do. Refuse anybody entrance to the house and shout through the door that you could clear off. That's what he did.'

'Why?'

'He got eccentric. I think he didn't want the family to know the state the farm was in and how poverty-stricken him and my aunt were living. After all, he'd been a proud man once.'

'Are the Quills an extensive family?'

'What do you mean? Are there a lot of us? Yes. Close and distant relations. I've two brothers, as you've probably already found out. Then Uncle Harry's wife has a lot of relatives, second cousins of ours and the like. I couldn't run through the lot, but there's plenty. If you attend the funeral tomorrow, you'll soon find out. There'll be a real turnout. Always is at a Quill funeral... Here, what's goin' on...?'

Jerry rushed into the open to investigate a closed van which was manoeuvring its way to the shed next door and finding some difficulty in getting round the inert steamroller standing like some fossilised relic of a former age at a short distance away. Cromwell left sitting on a hard wooden chair, heard harsh words being bandied about.

'Have you come for him?'

'Aye. Can't you shift this old roller? It's in our way.'

'Don't be daft! You need to get steam up to move that. You'll have to work round it. Why has it taken you so long to get on with the removal?'

'He's got to take his turn. This isn't the only corpse we've had to handle today, you know...'

Cromwell sauntered to the window to see what was going on.

The undertaker and his men were carrying a coffin into the morgue. Jerry, who was wearing a black felt hat, removed it reverently as the empty shell passed him. The mutes seemed to make quick work of the job, for they were back again in a few minutes, bearing the closed coffin and its burden in a very business-like fashion. Jerry stood rigid again with his hat extended, like a beggar soliciting alms. The undertakers shipped their load somewhat roughly in the van and closed the door. Jerry thought a protest against the irreverent handling was due.

'You might have been a bit more respectful to the dead. You're not loading potatoes, you know.'

'We're in a hurry. We'll give 'im the respect due to him in the proper place, in the funeral parlour. S'long.'

Jerry returned to his depot wearing a blank expression as though musing on what might happen to him when his time came.

'You still here?'

'Yes. I've one more question, when you've recovered sufficiently to answer it. Did any of your numerous relatives, on either your uncle's or your aunt's side, visit the farm frequently?'

'From what I hear, Evelyn, my aunt's niece, used to go to see her now and then when Uncle Harry wasn't at home. Evelyn was always one for the money. Insults or even violence wouldn't keep her away if there was money to be had. Anythin' else?'

There was a brief interruption caused by the arrival of a shabby man in a cloth cap and dungarees, who, without ceremony entered and flung a small bundle held together by a rubber band on Jerry's desk.

'Two dozen,' he said. 'Two pound eight…'

Cromwell with a squeamish spasm recognised the parcel as rats' tails.

'Knock when you come in 'ere. I'm busy now.'

'I'm not keepin' you. Give me the cash and I'll blow.'

Jerry handed over the money from a tin box in his drawer and put the grisly parcel away on an old biscuit tin on the floor nearby.

'We pay two bob for every rat's tail brought in,' he explained to Cromwell, as though the Inspector himself might have a few to dispose of.

The rodent officer's department seemed to be livening up, for two more workmen, again in caps and boiler suits and with their heavy boots clotted with earth, appeared in the doorway. One was old and bent; the other, loaded with cans, sacks and traps, a youth with a smiling vacant expression.

'We've finished at Johnson's warehouse. Fifty-three,' said the old 'un, giving the tally of his morning's hunting. 'We're goin' for us tea now.'

And they both withdrew.

So did Cromwell after thanking and bidding Mr. Jerry Quill good day. After a surfeit of corpses and rats, he didn't feel much like lunch. However… All in a day's work.

He lit a cigarette and made his way to the main gates, passing a small garden in which presumably were raised the shrubs and young trees for embellishing the streets and squares of the town. Seated beneath a large plane tree which had apparently been left behind to flourish to its heart's content, were the two rodent assistants of Mr. Jerry Quill.

They were comfortably spread on two large sacks and were eating their refreshments with great relish. The old man, large slabs of thickly buttered bread and an onion which he bit into like an apple; the young lost-looking assistant, three cornish pasties and a pile of iced buns. The old man greeted Cromwell as though he'd known him all his life.

'Got a chew of tobacco, sir?'

'No, sorry. Will a cigarette do?'

The old man agreed that it would. He had a fine pair of National Health dentures on the grass beside him. He politely put them in his pocket.

'Can't eat with 'em in,' he said apologetically. 'Jest wear 'em to improve me looks.'

Cromwell took a cigarette and lit it and then gave the old 'un the rest of the packet.

'You from the police? Been seein' Jerry about his uncle's death? I seen you goin' in the police station earlier in the day. Not much you'll get out of Jerry Quill. But he didn't kill his uncle. Couldn't even kill a rat proper, never mind a man...'

The old man, who later said his name was Alfred Jacques, Alf for short, seemed to have so much to say to Cromwell that he couldn't even wait for answers to his questions. Edward Douglas, Ted for short, took not the least interest in the encounter, but joyfully contemplated his pasties and iced buns and demolished them in two bites apiece like a friendly elephant.

'Don't think we suspect Mr. Quill. I only called to see him in view of his relationship with the dead man.'

Alf took a bite of his onion and two bites of his hunks of bread with his bare gums and paused to masticate and think. Then he emitted another string of observations.

'Now and then, Jerry Quill used to go to see his uncle on the farm. He pretended it was to see the place was free from rats. If that was his reason, why didn't he take me? Always went on his own. Jerry wouldn't know what to do with a rat if he saw one. He's scared of rats. All he does is enter 'em in a book, pay for rats' tails, answer the telephone and make his report once a month to the borough council. Me and Ted does all the work. He got the job because he married the daughter of the chairman of the 'ealth committee.'

Eating onions, smoking a cigarette and telling his tale, Alf had his hands and his mouth full. He paused to sort himself out.

'Why did Jerry go to Sprawle if it wasn't for rats and if his uncle wouldn't see him? It's said that not even his own kith and kin was allowed across the threshold of Great Lands farm. And why did Jerry go off in the van with a pick and spade and…?'

Alf paused to take a look at Ted, who was now fast asleep. He seemed satisfied that they weren't overheard and reduced his voice to a whisper.

'And why did he go when he knew his uncle wasn't there? Why did he? I ask you. Why did he?'

'Why did he?' repeated Cromwell.

'Don't ask me to do your work for you. I don't know. But I do know that three times when Jerry Quill told me he was goin' to Great Lands to make a rat inspection, I met his uncle in the mart, where I go ever market day to see there's no vermin around.'

'And you don't know why Jerry went to Sprawle. Perhaps it was to have a little private rehearsal at rat catching when nobody was about.'

'Not him. He never did no rat catching, nor intended to. But he went there while his uncle was with his fancy lady in the town.'

'What do you know about that, Alf?'

'Quite a lot. All the market men knew and laughed at him behind his back. Creepin' up to her room when he thought nobody was lookin'. I could tell you a thing or two about those two. I seen them at it and it wasn't what you think...'

He paused and lit another cigarette.

'Look here. You've been very decent with me. If I tell you somethin', will you promise not to tell who told you? Will you?'

'Very good. I'll promise.'

'I said I'd seen Harry Quill and Rosie at it, didn't I? Well, I did. I was up a ladder and saw it all through the window. Now if you was to tell anybody what I'm tellin' you, I'd lose me job for spying on people in the course of my duties and talking about 'em. So, you see...'

'I do.'

Cromwell, feeling at a disadvantage towering above Alf's reclining figure, arranged a spare sack on the grass and, after making sure there were no rats in it, squatted on it beside the rat-catcher. The three of them, two sitting cross-legged and another fast asleep, looked like members of an opium-smoking party.

'Well... the building that Rosie has her room in belongs to the Marcroft corporation, who rent it to the tobacconist in the shop and he lets off the little flats upstairs. It's old and the corporation bought it for demolition some day when they've the money to do it. It's very old and it got beetles and woodworm in the rafters. I was sent to inspect it and then clear up the rafters, paint 'em with pest killer and leave all neat and tidy again. I was there three weeks and was inspecting the roof from a ladder outside, when climbing past Rosie's window, I couldn't help seeing what went on inside...'

No doubt the old rascal played Peeping Tom wherever his work gave him a chance and Cromwell, watching his crafty face, was sure he'd timed his ladder climbing to coincide with Harry Quill's furtive visits there.

'Saw them together three times. They didn't see me, I'm sure of that, because I didn't put the ladder going past the window in case I broke some glass. I was just round the side and could peep in...'

The old man was enjoying himself. He giggled and then exposed his toothless mouth in a wild laugh.

'Where do you think they were? Not where you think. Not in bed. Where?'

'You tell me.'

'Sittin' at a table on two chairs talking pleasantly together as happy as a pair could be. Do you know why Harry Quill was visitin' Rosie in secret? Eh? I'll tell you. Harry was a teetotaller. All the market knew that. He'd once knocked a man down for trying to get him to take a drink and then insultin' him for not doing. Harry daren't let himself down by drinking at the bar of a pub, or at home, or anywhere where he'd be seen and be mocked for breaking the pledge. It would have been a great joke. When I saw Harry and Rosie they were drinkin' stout. Harry was a secret drinker, you see, and Rosie was helpin' him.'

'When was this?'

'A bit over a year ago, I was on the job.'

What an anti-climax! Cromwell felt disgusted at the banality of the affair. He regretted the time he'd wasted in the sordid little world of Jerry Quill.

Cromwell boiled over. He'd already had enough of Jerry and his staff.

'Talkin' of drinkin' stout...'

Cromwell took the hint, gave the old man half a crown and left him. He stood, undecided for a minute before he left the yard and then turned and walked back.

The door of Jerry Quill's office was still ajar and Cromwell pushed it open. Quill was inside, eating cake at his desk and drinking tea from a vacuum flask. He looked annoyed.

'You here again. I'm having my tea break and it's not fair to intrude on my time off.'

'I'm back because you didn't tell me a full story about Harry Quill. In the course of our enquiries, we've been told that you have been in the habit of calling at Great Lands during Harry Quill's absence in Marcroft. Is that so?'

'Who told you that? Even if I did find my uncle out, there was nothing wrong in that. I'd gone to enquire about vermin in the place. It was neglected and just inviting rats and other pests. I found him out once and that didn't interfere with my work. I just let my aunt know I was there and then I got on with the job.'

'But you were alone. Don't you usually take your workmen with you on an exploration of that kind?'

Jerry was so put out that he overturned his flask and flooded the top of his desk.

'Now look what you've done,' he whimpered.

He rushed around, seeking cloths to mop it up and then he meticulously dried it, without even a look at Cromwell.

Cromwell was waiting for him.

'Well?'

'Well, what?'

'You went to Great Lands alone. Your staff generally accompanied you on such trips elsewhere, didn't they?'

'I'm not answerable to the police for family visits and you've no right...'

'Don't dodge the issue, sir.'

'I'm not doing. I was there on public business.'

'With a pick and spade. Were you going to dig them out yourself?'

'If necessary, yes.'

All the same, his confidence had evaporated and his eyes were shifty, almost appealing.

'You're still withholding information, Mr. Quill. You're obstructing the police and that's a grave offence, especially coming from a public servant. I'd be very loath to report it, as it may cost you your job. We're here helping the county police and if they heard of your attitude, it would certainly prejudice your reputation locally.'

Which was going rather far, but Cromwell was determined to get to the root of Quill's attitude.

Quill shuffled about on his chair.

'What do you want to know? You seem to think I'm in possession of some secret information about Uncle Harry. I know nothing that anybody else doesn't know.'

'I can't understand your visits to Great Lands during your uncle's absence. You went alone, without your workmen. Surely, if you were after vermin, you'd have gone when your uncle was there to show you round. Instead, you went, on your own, with a pick and shovel. What were you intending to do in his absence? Give me a straight answer.'

Quill's face grew white. He felt he could do with a drink, but he daren't be seen taking it whilst on duty. He was obviously a heavy drinker. The strain of the interview and the weariness due to steering a cautious course had given him a besotted look.

Finally, he gave in.

'Well, it was this way. My cousin Evelyn was the only one of the family who ever got in the house. She was my aunt's favourite and went to see her when Uncle Harry was on business in Marcroft. One day Evelyn met my wife in town and in the course of conversation said her aunt had told her she was sure Uncle had money hidden somewhere. My aunt had searched the house for it, but there wasn't a trace...'

'Hold on a minute, Mr. Quill. I thought your aunt was incapacitated and almost unable to move about the place at all.'

'That's what everybody else thought. Evelyn said that when she was alone, my aunt moved about the place, upstairs and down. She must have done it on her hands and knees, or something, and it must have been a 'orrible effort for her, but Evelyn, though she'd never seen her doing it, knew from the things she said, that Aunt was aware of all that went on in the house.'

'I see. Did Harry Quill know that?'

'Don't ask me. I don't know. I never talked with him. But, as I was saying, my aunt talked of Harry having money hidden somewhere and, for her sake, because he was living on her money, I thought I'd try to find out where it was hid.'

'So, you went digging?'

'What! On a five hundred acre farm? I'm not mad. No. I took the tools to make it look as if I was there on business. Then, I took a good look round in all the buildings and other likely places. I never found anything.'

Cromwell knew it was a lie. Jerry was too glib once he'd got in his stride. As he warmed up in his story, he began to embellish it. He lost his furtive expression as he thought Cromwell was swallowing it all.

'There are two old wells there. It might have been hidden in one of them. I'd no means of findin' out. And there were all the stables and cowsheds, all tumbling down with the roofs full of holes. They were full of rubbish and rubble. I couldn't shift that. I had to give it up.'

Cromwell saw that he'd have to give it up, too. Jerry Quill had been up to something, but he wasn't going to say what.

It might have been that he was spying on Evelyn, whom he seemed to dislike very heartily, because she was probably in line for the meagre inheritance her aunt would leave behind.

Or Jerry might have been hanging round the place trying, some way, to restore himself to his aunt's favour in the hope of winning a share of her estate.

'One last question. Do you know anybody who might have hated your uncle enough to want to kill him?'

Jerry looked appalled.

'Certainly not. He was disliked, but you don't murder a chap because he's rude to you or you don't like his way of living. Besides, who'd want to kill him to inherit a tumble-down old farm with all the land in bad heart and some of it swamp and wilderness? It would cost a fortune to restore it.'

'You seem to have sized everything up properly, Mr. Quill.'

'Look here. I think you've been here long enough. And now that you've started bein' offensive, it's time you went.'

'Where were you on the night your uncle died?'

'Are you treatin' me as a suspect, because, if you are ...'

'Purely routine for the record.'

'Well, I was at my lodge meetin' in Marcroft from seven till eleven. Any of my brother members'll tell you that. After the meetin', I went home. Ask the wife if you doubt my word. And now, I'm off for a drink. I need it after all you've said to me. I hope when you catch whoever killed my uncle, you'll have the grace to call on me again and apologise for your unfair insinuations. Come on, I want to lock up the office.'

'By the way, where can I find your brother, Herbert, in case I want to ask him any questions?'

Jerry snorted.

'In the Marcroft General Hospital. He's been there three weeks with a coronary thrombosis. So, he wasn't abroad by night when Uncle Harry was killed. I'm sure you'll be welcome at the hospital if you want to pester him with questions like you've done me. He'll have another attack.'

Cromwell left him locking up.

Chapter VI
Stillwaters

It was dusk, after a long day, when Littlejohn and Cromwell, having dined early, started out for Branscombe to see Timothy Quill. The village lay about ten miles west of Marcroft, through open country and was approached by Branscombe Forest, to which it owed its name. Lights were beginning to show in farms and houses as they neared the place.

Tim Quill had chosen a good spot in which to make his home. The two detectives passed through the forest itself as, according to the map at the police station, the farm, known as Stillwaters, stood on the edge of it.

The last stretch of road ran through a wall of trees, the summits of which met above the twin grass verges and the highway seemed to unfold onwards in mysterious semi-darkness.

Their knock on the large, nail-studded door of Stillwaters was answered by a woman. She had switched on a light over the porch and it seemed to exaggerate her hollow cheeks and prominent cheek bones. Her pale face was without expression and her raised eyebrows alone questioned the visitors and their purpose.

'Is Mr. Quill at home?'

She smiled with her lips.

'I am Mrs. Quill. Can I help?'

Littlejohn introduced himself and Cromwell.

'It is about Mr. Quill's uncle?'

'Yes.'

'Then I'll find him. He is somewhere in the stables making plans for the shooting season with a friend, who hopes to try out a new dog...'

There seemed to be little purpose in the explanation, but it might have arisen from nervousness about the coming interview.

She invited them in and led the way to a fine room dominated by a huge Welsh dresser with expensive china spread on the shelves. The whole place was elegant in chintz and old oak. A refectory table was set ready for a meal and an old dog lay stretched before the fire in a large open grate. There seemed to be nobody about; not a sound came from anywhere in the house, except when there was a lull in the talk, they could hear a clock ticking in the hall.

'I'll find him.'

She wore a tweed skirt and a white blouse with a pale blue cardigan over it. She was dark and her short black hair was touched with grey and left the back of her shapely neck uncovered. In the shaded light which treated her face more mercifully than the stark lamp over the outer door, she was strikingly beautiful. The emaciated look had gone, but under her dark eyes were the careworn shadows of unhappiness.

'Please be seated. Will you take a drink whilst I find him?'

She gave them whisky and cigarettes and then left them. They did not see her again that night.

The place was either a renovated old one or else someone, presumably Timothy Quill, had started from scratch.

There was a lot of newness about the house. Fittings, central heating equipment, expensive metal fireplace, polished floor with Persian mats scattered on it made it less like a farmhouse and more like a country retreat of some opulent city commuter. Outside, too, from what they had seen in the half darkness of coming night, the buildings had the look of an orderly, well-run factory, ranged in a precise square behind the house. Someone had casually said in the course of the enquiry that Timothy Quill had done well for himself. He had been bailiff at a farm, miles away, owned by a wealthy county wholesale grocer and had married his master's daughter. This set-up was the obvious result.

There was a small round oak table between the chairs occupied by Littlejohn and Cromwell and there were a few country magazines and social periodicals on it. Cromwell leaned and looked them over and finally took up a foolscap size leather-bound book and casually turned over the pages. He raised his eyebrows and passed it to Littlejohn.

It was a modern version of a family album with photographs in it. The first few pages were concerned with the erection of Stillwaters. An old building, little more than a country cottage, with a few outhouses. Then the bare site. And then the gradual erection of the new farm itself. Several pictures of a garden party and some dogs. There were no children about. In a family as prolific as the Quills, this seemed strange. Perhaps it was explained by the blank spaces whence several photographs had been removed, like those, in days past, of the family rakes and remittance-men withdrawn after their misbehaviour and banished forever.

Footsteps sounded heavily from the rear and then Timothy Quill appeared in the doorway. He was the type who, according to the talk of the Quills about pride and the one-time manor house state of affairs at Sprawle, ought to have been the lord of Great Lands.

In his youth, he must have cut a fine figure. Now, nearer fifty than forty, he had run to seed. He still had a good head of dark curly hair, now tufted at the sides with grey, but it had grown thin and showed his scalp through it, and had been carefully brushed over bald patches. His nose had thickened and the bone structure of his face, once triangular with a long pointed chin, had accumulated the bloated flesh of good living. He was still straight, six feet tall and heavy. He was wearing well-polished gumboots and a dark pullover and grey flannel trousers tucked in the boots. He stood for a moment in the doorway, frowning, one hand shading his eyes from the sudden light.

'This is a late hour for police business, isn't it?'

Littlejohn apologised. They had been fully occupied in Marcroft all day, he said. They would not take much of Mr. Quill's time.

Quill nodded that he accepted the excuse and crossed to the whisky bottle and helped himself to a stiff drink and shot in a little soda. Another member of the family who had broken the traditional pledge against what they called strong drink.

'Either of you have another?'

They thanked him and declined.

'Well, let's get on with it. I can't think what you want to ask me that will help you solve this crime. I see from the evening paper that it wasn't committed by the gang who were robbing farmhouses. Or, at least, not by the black gang. It might have been done by another crowd imitating them. That sort of crime spreads. It's so easy.'

'You may be right. All the same, we must investigate every avenue ...'

'Well, I haven't even got an avenue. I don't see how I can help at all.'

'I hear you and your late uncle got on very well.'

'Where did you hear that? We never quarrelled, if that's what you mean, but we weren't in any way buddies. We rarely met. I never visited Great Lands. It turned my stomach, as a practical farmer, to see the place in such a shocking condition. It was our old family home, but had no sentimental ties for me. I suppose there's a sense of property in the Quill blood, but that sort of property has no appeal to me. My uncle ought to have been hanged for letting it get into such a condition, though. And yet...'

He paused and looked hard at the glass in his hand. He rose and refilled it.

'And yet... I couldn't help feeling sorry for the old man. Do you know how much he paid for the two hundred acres his father sold to pay off his stupid debts. Five thousand pounds!'

He looked at them both to see their astonishment at the news and when they didn't seem surprised, he shouted it again.

'Five thousand pounds! Wilderness, it was. Valueless almost. And he left himself without a cent to restore it. He must have gone off his head.'

Littlejohn shrugged his shoulders.

'I must confess, sir, that whenever we try to talk about Harry Quill, the state of the farm and the lost two hundred acres seems to dominate everything. As far as the discovery of who committed the murder goes, the farm itself and the land Harry Quill bought back are red herrings. We want to know had Harry Quill any enemies. Had he anybody who hated him so much that they'd go to his farm and strike him down in the night, with nobody but a helpless wife to witness the scene and call pathetically for help by firing a haystack to which she must have had to crawl across the farmyard? That effort killed her. She died without recovering consciousness. The murderer has two crimes on his conscience, if he has any conscience at all.'

'You talk about discovering who committed the crime. I suppose you think that if it wasn't the work of one of those gangs of hooligans, somebody in the family did it. Am I right?'

'We've formed no ideas or theories yet. We're just beginning the investigation.'

Tim Quill took another good drink. He did it eagerly as though seeking some kind of inspiration in it instead of quenching his thirst.

'All the same, you're doubtless thinking somebody in the family might have done it with a view to benefiting from Harry's will? That's true, isn't it?'

'That type of motive always has to be taken into account. Why?'

'Because there's no sense in it in this case. Have you seen Great Lands and the farmhouse property? A dead house, like an empty sepulchre. And five hundred acres of desert. No money with which to run it…'

'How do you know that?'

'Uncle Harry was dead broke after he bought the last of the land his father had sold. He needed capital to carry on with and he just hadn't got any. Aunt Millicent had a little money of her own, but wouldn't part with any of it. I don't blame her. Uncle Harry made the rounds of the banks and finance offices, but they wouldn't play. Great Lands farm was just a write-off as security. They'd have been mad to advance a bean against it. So Harry tried the family. He came to me. He told me the full story. He couldn't justify the purchase of the land his father had sold in any practical way. All he could say over and over again, was that it was *his*, and he'd promised his father on his deathbed that he'd get it back again. And he was determined to have it back. He was mad. He just *wanted* it, like a child crying for something that takes his fancy. What he was going to do with it when once he'd got it, didn't seem to matter. All he could do, in the circumstances, was just to sit and watch it go wilder than it already was.'

'You refused to help?'

'Of course I did. I've got a good set-up here, but I'm fully extended and haven't any cash to spare. To throw my resources away on that sort of folly would have been lunacy.'

'Did your uncle say what he proposed to do after you'd refused him?'

'He said he'd have to try others in the family.'

'Your brothers?'

Quill laughed unpleasantly.

'Have you met them?'

'Inspector Cromwell has interviewed Gerald. I haven't met either of them. Your other brother has been in hospital for three weeks, I hear.'

'Yes. They haven't two sixpences to rub together between them. My uncle despised them. Called them a pair of twerps. He certainly had no intention of asking them for assistance.'

'Who then?'

'Probably Aunt Clara. She's the wealthiest of the lot of us. She's my great aunt, really, and a widow. She's eighty.'

'Tell us about her.'

The old dog on the hearth, which had slept through everything like a dead thing, now began to twitch and yap in his dreams. Quill crossed and gently patted and comforted him and he stretched himself and settled again.

'Aunt Clara is the widow of Algernon Quill. Algie, for short. He was a little tinpot corn-merchant in Marcroft when he married Aunt Clara. He was what you'd call a fancy-man. All dressed up to the nines, with his hair pomaded and plastered down and his moustache waxed. He had a way with the ladies. She was a school teacher and turned out to be a fine business woman. After the marriage, I gather, she handled all the business and Algie became a kind of drone. When he died, about thirty years ago, they owned between them three shops, a corn mill, four large farms, and a whole lot of house property. They occupied a nice Georgian house in Longton Curlieu, about ten miles south of Marcroft, and my aunt still lives there. They had a staff of servants and a carriage and pair, later to be replaced by a Rolls Royce, in which Aunt Clara will probably arrive at tomorrow's funeral. It's now a vintage model. Until he died, Algie used to be seen regularly in Marcroft, with a flower in his buttonhole, ogling all the girls just like the man who broke the bank at Monte Carlo. Aunt sold out most of her enterprises years ago and therefore must have plenty of ready money.'

'Did Harry approach her?'

'I guess he did. I can't be sure. But the answer was obvious from the state Great Lands remained in. I saw Harry a time or two in the mart at Marcroft after that, but he never said anything about his money affairs. I didn't ask. As for Aunt Clara, she doesn't associate much with the Quills. I don't blame her. We'll all be seeing her, though, tomorrow at Harry's and Millie's funerals. She attends all the family burials.'

'Will you be there?'

'Of course. Nunn, the lawyer, is officially in charge and has advised all the family of arrangements. It's like an edict. If I don't attend, I'll have half the family calling here to know the reason why. Wanting to know if I'm sick or something…God knows why this family spirit keeps so many incongruous people hanging together, but it does. I'll have to show up to keep those I don't want from my doorstep. My wife won't be going, of course, and there'll be an inquisition about that, too.'

'Was Harry friendly with all of them?'

'Not a bit of it. If any of them turned up at Great Lands, he kept them standing at the door and soon gave them a rude hint that they'd better push off. And yet, if I'd died before him, he'd have been at the cemetery with all the rest to see me laid away and throw dust on my coffin.'

'So, you'd say that though he kept his relatives at arm's length, Harry Quill never hurt them so much that they'd want to kill him for the affront?'

'Certainly they wouldn't want to kill him. Any of the Quills murdering Harry is unthinkable. As a matter of fact, he was quite a family character. He and Aunt Clara were the eccentrics of the Quills, and I don't need to tell you that such oddities become legendary among their relatives and exaggerated tales are bandied about concerning them. They create a sort of family pride and envy by their behaviour. After Aunt Clara's phenomenal appearance tomorrow, when she'll only speak to one or two chosen ones, in spite of the obsequious efforts of all the rest, the family will remember her antics and take pleasure in reminding one another of what she did and said.'

Cromwell smiled to himself, thinking of his great-aunt Lucy, who ran away with a married man, a porter on Rugby station, who had fallen for her as he carried her bags from the Peterborough to the Crewe train.

'Do you know Rosie Coggins?'

Littlejohn changed the subject so suddenly that Tim Quill was taken aback. His lips moved, but no words came. He sat upright and swallowed a large drink and then slowly placed his glass on the table.

'What are you getting at?'

The conversation, from being good humoured, seemed to have taken a nasty turn now.

'You know, I suppose, that Harry Quill and Rose were good friends?'

'I've heard it talked about in the cattle market, but regarded it as bawdy gossip of the sort that flourishes there.'

'It was true. We've confirmed it. They met frequently in her flat where, it seems, Harry used to retire and drink the stout he was ashamed to consume in public.'

'What does Rose Coggins have to say about it? I suppose you've asked her?'

'Do you know her?'

'As barmaid at the *Drovers Inn*, that's all. What had she to say about Uncle Harry?'

He persisted angrily in his question, as though family pride were rising again.

'She didn't deny the rumour. He visited her for a friendly chat, a bottle of stout, and nothing else, she said.'

'Nothing wrong in that, is there?'

'No. But some people refuse to believe that it ended there.'

'But that's ridiculous. A barmaid!'

Again! As though Harry had been a wealthy lord of the manor, instead of a bankrupt farmer, living on his wife's income, dressed in old clothes, cloth cap and muddy boots and without a collar, a brass-topped stud glistening in the neckband of his shirt.

'Why ridiculous? Rose seemed to think he was a gentleman for all his rough appearance and in spite of his poverty.'

'I'm glad to hear that! Even if it did come from the barmaid of a two-bit pub.'

Then, suddenly, he thought of something else.

'He hasn't made a will in her favour, has he?'

'You'll know the answer tomorrow when the will is read. I suppose wills are read at the family gatherings.'

'You know! And he *has* been up to something in his will, hasn't he?'

Tim Quill was quite upset. He filled up his glass again without offering more to the other two, and drank heavily.

'I'll be damned! Now what's going to happen? I'll have to see Nunn before that will is read. She's not getting away with this.'

'You'd better be quite sure Rose is involved before you start behaving like a bull in a china shop, sir.'

No reply. Quill was too obsessed by his thoughts and a new horror in the situation. He wanted to be rid of his visitors.

'Is that all? I want to think this all out before I go to bed. I'll have to be in Nunn's office good and early tomorrow. The funeral's at eleven!'

It seemed a thin sort of dismissal but there was no point in staying on.

'One final question, sir. Where were you on the night your uncle died?'

Quill looked alarmed.

'You surely don't think I killed him?'

'Just routine, sir.'

'I was at a meeting of the Farmers' Union in Marcroft till eleven o'clock. Then I took a friend home. He lives a mile from here on the road to town. We'd a few drinks there and parted at one o'clock. Will that suit you?'

'Quite well, thank you.'

They bade him good night. He hardly seemed aware they were going.

Mist was drifting up from the fields as they left and obscuring the lights dotted in the darkness. Somewhere a dog was barking.

In the front windows of an upper room of the farmhouse lights were still burning. It must have been Mrs. Tim Quill, who had looked at the end of her tether and empty of all hope, waiting anxiously to know why the police had been there so long.

Chapter VII
Gathering of the Clan

'Who are those two men? Are they reporters? We don't want any intruders.'

Aunt Clara descended from her ancient car assisted by Mr. Nunn. They were the last to arrive and now the process of interring Harry Quill and his wife could proceed.

She pointed an ebony walking stick, with a large rubber ferrule on the business end of it, at Littlejohn and Cromwell, modestly watching in the shade of a huge marble monument denoting the last resting place of a former mayor of Marcroft. His period of office had been marked by the bulldozing down of the town centre and its re-erection, and his record on the memorial slab ended 'Peace, perfect Peace.'

'They're the detectives from London investigating Harry's death.'

Aunt Clara screwed her lips tightly and then opened them briskly again with a noise like a popping champagne cork.

'Tell them right away I wish to see them after the funeral. They'd better join us at the *Marcroft Arms* for coffee.'

Mr. Nunn hesitated, as the proceedings had been held up long enough. Some of the family had been at the graveside for an hour or more, not quite knowing why they were there so early, but attracted like the crowd at a coronation or a football match.

'Be off with you, Nunn. I'll wait for you...'

Which meant they'd all wait. So, the lawyer delivered the message.

Everybody was dressed in black. Some of the men, bolder than the rest, had put on coloured pullovers under their coats, but changed their attitudes when faced by the family phalanx and had buttoned their jackets to conceal their finery. Those who had grown too large for their ceremonial suits were now deeply waisted and out of shape like large, distorted hour-glasses, as the buttons bit into their paunches.

Many had come from distant parts. William Quill, a cousin of the dead man and usually known as Bill Quill, had even travelled from some remote spot in the south, seventy miles away, by motor-cycle, bringing with him his wife and family in a sidecar resembling a sedan chair. He had received an ovation as he eased his huge, pneumatic wife, panting for breath, from the sedan followed by a huge wreath and three children, one of whom he allowed to follow her mother and the other two, after hitting them each on the head, he impounded in the sidecar. His cap was back to front when he showed up and this he respectfully turned round to normal before he joined his tribe.

Aunt Clara wore black, too, stockings and gloves and all, and a misshapen black felt hat squashed on her head. A small thin woman, very upright still, her face was brown and shrivelled like an old walnut, and her prominent scythe of a nose and pointed chin struggled to meet over her thin colourless lips.

The lot of them looked incongruous in the bright sunshine. Mr. Nunn was the only impeccable one among them;

they were awkward and ill dressed. There was a prevailing smell of mothballs and Jerry Quill, who had already risked a few quick drinks, was chewing a clove in case his Aunt Clara got too near him.

A few sightseers gathered round to watch and included a number of men from the mart dressed in their working clothes.

With the exception of Tim and Jerry, Littlejohn didn't know any of them. Big Quills and little Quills, near and distant nephews and nieces and cousins. One overblown and fertile looking woman had three children hanging round her skirts.

'I hadn't anybody to leave them with,' she explained to her neighbours, *sotto voce,* which resounded round the group. They all seemed anxious to emphasise the trouble they'd taken to be there.

Aunt Clara looked round with a sort of objective curiosity, as though mentally calling the family roll. Then she broke through the throng. The Quills fell back, greeting her shyly without receiving any replies, and she hobbled her way to the graveside followed by the nonchalant lawyer. Tim Quill edged to her side. He was dressed in a black suit, too, which he had outgrown a little, and he carried a black bowler hat, the only one there.

'No scenes, please,' said Aunt Clara to Mr. Nunn as though she expected him to translate it in legal form and convey it to the rest.

The relatives gathered round roughly in order of blood relationship – *per stirpes,* as Mr. Nunn would have had it in drawing up a will.

Whilst all this was going on, the hearses had arrived, followed by two taxis and a van. The taxis poured out Mr. Bilbow, who seemed to be the major-domo of the event, the undertaker, four mutes, and a tall, flabby man with a bilious face covered with stiff little white bristles; Pastor Mole, the minister of an obscure and declining denomination to which the Quills owed nominal allegiance. The driver of the van opened the doors and began to take out wreaths and spread them on a large grass plot nearby. Littlejohn thought it was never going to end. In the distance, under a weeping willow which almost spread its leaves down to her waist, he recognised Rose Coggins. She was dabbing her eyes with a handkerchief screwed in a ball in her fist.

It all went along smoothly. The coffins were brought along consecutively, very plain, which seemed to annoy certain of the mourners, who thought they might have been a bit more ornamental, instead of like paupers' boxes. Mr. Mole took a long time. It wasn't often he presided over such a large throng and he made the most of it. Finally, with a gesture, he divided the living from the dead and there was a rush to the wreaths to make sure that they'd all arrived and to compare one with another.

Mr. Bilbow joined his master and Aunt Clara, taking care to place a considerable distance between himself and the old lady. He had been tippling a bit before the funeral and his eyes sparkled through his beard. Nunn gestured to Littlejohn and Cromwell to join them. Rose Coggins had melted away.

Littlejohn and Cromwell were to meet Aunt Clara at the *Marcroft Arms* immediately after the funeral. There was to be the usual feast of mourners at an unlicensed eating-house in the town. Mr. Bilbow was in charge of that, too. He stayed behind with the rest whilst Aunt Clara and Mr. Nunn went off in her large barouche. She didn't invite Littlejohn and Cromwell to join them in the vehicle. It was like a royal funeral where everybody is strictly kept in place.

Littlejohn could imagine all the Quills swarming in the café, where presumably, the feast would be provided at the expense of Millicent Quill's estate. Harry hadn't left any money for junketing. It looked as if Millicent's money would have to cover her husband's funeral as well.

He could see in his mind's eye, too, the shabby café set out with plates of ham or beef for the meal. No alcoholic drinks, of course. In the financial circumstances they might have to be content with water. They'd all start milling about, sorting themselves out into groups of friends and near relatives, discussing Harry Quill and his wife and the mysteries of their deaths and then going on to events which had happened in the family, years, perhaps centuries ago. A teetotal feast.

Of course, there'd be some there who would sneak off and have a little tipple on the sly after the meal. Bilbow, for example. And Tim and Jerry. They were the kind who feel the need of stimulants after the grim, mournful boring ceremonies and company of such a gathering. Some of the Quills had openly kicked over the traces. Jerry, for instance. Everybody knew he took to the bottle. He'd drunk himself into D.T.s twice according to local records and had almost lost his job. If his wife's father hadn't been a big shot, an alderman on the town council, Jerry would have got the sack right away.

And Harry... The man who'd boasted of his family, and his temperance ancestors and had once owned a chapel. Something had happened to Harry which changed his life. He'd started to slip. First the farm; he'd begun to neglect that. Then he'd become a complete recluse and refused to see any of his once precious Quill relatives. He'd pulled down the chapel and patched up his house with the slates from the roof. And finally, in his late middle-age, he'd broken the pledge and started toping himself. Only a single bottle of stout, according to Rosie Coggins, but it might have been more than that. He'd gone further, too. After a life of fidelity to his wife, albeit she was a helpless invalid, he'd struck up an acquaintance with a barmaid. Rosie had said it was just a platonic affair. But was it? Harry had been steadily on the decline. Had he gone the limit there, too, and broken another pledge?

'I shan't be going to the vulgar meal at Bennings' Café. The Quills are nothing to me. I've brought sandwiches which I shall eat in the car in a quiet spot on the way home. You can order coffee at the hotel and pay for it out of the funeral expenses. It will cost the estate far less than if I'd joined the rest and eaten a full meal which would certainly have made me ill afterwards...'

Aunt Clara had worked it out to the last penny, it seemed. Mr. Nunn smiled wearily and made the arrangements. Littlejohn found them at the hotel. On second thoughts he'd sent Cromwell with the main body of mourners to join the feast. There would be talk there which might reveal some family secrets. Nunn was looking bored to death and Aunt Clara annoyed because the police had kept her waiting. She had a glass of brandy with the coffee. She'd complained of fatigue. She wasn't one of the family who hid her tastes and, after all, it was a medicinal draught and Mrs. Harry Quill's little nest-egg was paying the bill.

'Sit down. Your coffee's cold, but you'll have to make do with it.'

Nunn shrugged his shoulders gently at Littlejohn, to let him know that the reception was none of his doing. They were established in one corner of the lounge. It was lunch time and guests on their ways to the dining-room kept calling in for drinks before the meal. Some of them obviously knew Clara Quill and nodded or spoke without receiving any acknowledgement. The look she gave anyone who came within yards of their table ensured that their little conference would remain undisturbed.

Aunt Clara came right to the point.

'Where's the other man? There were two of you at the funeral!'

'He has other business in hand and asks to be excused.'

That was a good one! Cromwell, on receiving his orders to join the funeral junketing, had grinned, saying 'My God!' and then, somehow, become immersed in a riot of handshaking from those who mistook him for some obscure Quill from a remote place.

'You haven't, as yet, I presume, found out who killed Harry Quill?'

'Not yet, er...Mrs. Quill.'

He almost said Aunt Clara. Littlejohn felt he'd half joined the family himself, thinking of and discussing the members by their Christian names and seeming to be taking no liberties in accepting Aunt Clara as a relative like the rest.

'I hear you started on the wrong track and thought he'd been killed by the gang it took the police so long to apprehend. And now, you've to begin all over again.'

She smacked her lips as though the whole unhappy exercise pleased her.

'Whom do you suspect now?'

'We've no idea yet.'

'Nor ever will have at the rate you're going. You seem to be taking your time about everything. Was there any need for you to attend the funeral this morning?'

'We have our own methods and routine in conducting enquiries of this kind, Mrs. Quill. We shall pursue them as we think best.'

She actually smiled. A grim mirthless sort of affair, but a signal that when she couldn't get her own way and bully people about, she began to appreciate them.

'You are *the* Littlejohn, I presume?'

'I'm Chief Superintendent Littlejohn, yes.'

'I've heard of you. I don't miss much.'

She didn't explain what she meant.

'I've told Nunn there will not be any reading of the wills in front of the assembled relatives. They'll be disappointed, but anyone concerned can call and see Nunn about it. Bilbow will tell them that and spoil their appetites for the funeral feast. I asked you to call here to see me to inform you that there won't be anything left in Harry's estate. Not even the farm and lands. I have a mortgage over the property.'

Nunn shrugged his shoulders languidly at Littlejohn again, just to excuse himself for not already telling him. He'd had his orders beforehand and Mrs. Clara Quill was a very good client of Nunn and Co.

'I am anxious to help the police in their efforts, although, as you say, you have your own methods and don't need any help...'

'I didn't say that, Mrs. Quill. If you are in possession of any facts which will help us in the investigation, it is your duty to disclose them. That is the position.'

'You don't need to tell me that. I had an idea that you might visit Nunn and pump him about family matters. I forbade him to disclose anything until I had seen you myself. Now I will tell you about the mortgage, if you'll listen. Get some more coffee, Nunn, and another brandy. It's past my meal time and I'm fatigued.'

Nunn flicked his fingers at the waitress and ordered the drinks.

'I'd better get on. I want to be away before the family begin to disperse all over the town. You know Harry Quill suffered from a silly obsession of restoring to Great Lands the fields which his father sold to pay his gaming debts... Yes; he gambled on the Stock Exchange. He was a fool... You know all that.'

'Yes.'

'Who told you?'

'That is our business, madam. What you tell us will be treated with similar discretion.'

'Dear me! You are very secretive. However... when Harry had paid for the land he'd no money left with which to work it. He tried everywhere to raise a loan. His wife would not advance him anything, and quite right too. He was a bigger fool even than his father in financial matters. Nobody, including Nunn, would assist him. He finally came to me, expecting, I'm sure, to be shown the door. Instead, I arranged to lend him two thousand pounds against a mortgage of the entire property and land of Great Lands. He agreed. He said even if the mortgage had to be foreclosed some time, the place would still be in the family. Nunn handled it all; Harry took his cash; and that was that. I contend that the whole of the farm isn't worth half the amount, but I propose to take it over, have it worked, repaired, and put in good heart. Then, I shall dispose of it. It will pass from the Quills for ever. They have deserved to lose it.'

Nunn actually gave Littlejohn a sly wink and Littlejohn knew what it was all about. Farms were in big demand locally and eventually Aunt Clara would sell at a nice profit. However, Great Lands didn't look worth much at present and she'd get the lot on her mortgage.

'Now this is what I want to tell you...'

Aunt Clara's jaws were the only part of her face which moved. Her malicious little eyes were still and dead looking. She kept her head fixed and she faced Littlejohn rigidly as she spoke, as though she were pronouncing a death sentence on someone.

'Harry didn't use a cent of that loan on improving the farm. He either hid the money somewhere or else spent it. I believe he did the latter. He was keeping another woman!'

She spat it out, turned to her brandy and drank it off in a quick draught.

'How do you know that, Mrs. Quill?'

'I know all that goes on in the Quill family. I pay for the information. They are a weak lot. I know. I was married to one of them for thirty years. Any of their antics, disgraces, unseemly doings are reported to me. I, unfortunately, bear their name, and if there's any Quill mud flying, it finds its way in my direction. I've no intention that it shall stick on me. I keep abreast with what they're all up to.'

'Mr. Nunn?'

'Tell him, Nunn.'

Nunn made a half despairing gesture with a languid hand.

'That is so. I seem to bear the whole Quill clan on my shoulders...'

'And are well paid for it, Nunn.'

'I agree. Though I can't claim to do the detective work in this case. Bilbow is the Sherlock Holmes who produces all the unsavoury information.'

'And Bilbow discovered about Harry Quill's other woman?'

'Yes.'

'We know about Rose Coggins, of course.'

'That's nothing to boast about. Everybody knows. Harry thought they didn't, but even his wife knew. Now, if you knew who killed Harry and what happened to the money he borrowed from me, that would be a feather in your cap.'

'That's what we're here to find out, Mrs. Quill.'

'I hope you succeed. If it's one of the family who did it, I want him or her plucked out and destroyed. There's no place among the Quills for murderers. If the murderer isn't laid by the heels, he might try to make me his next victim. And besides, I want to know what's become of my two thousand pounds. I didn't go to all that trouble to have my capital stolen and dissipated prodigally...'

'Was it actually in cash?'

'Yes. Harry had no banking account, he said. I didn't know whether or not to believe him, but I got cash for him from the bank and gave it to him.'

'Have you any ideas about what happened to the money?'

She gave him a sly smile and closed her fingers firmly over the ivory handle of her ebony walking-stick. Her face was like a death's head.

'That is your business. But there is one thing to remember. Five people knew that Harry mortgaged his farm to me and had two thousand in cash at his disposal. You can count them on the fingers of one hand. Myself, of course; Nunn and his acolyte, Bilbow. Then, possibly the Coggins woman to whom he presumably opened his heart. And now, you. Five of us. You and I certainly didn't kill him for his money. That leaves Nunn, Bilbow and the woman.'

Nunn smiled wearily again. He seemed used to this sort of talk. He just tapped Aunt Clara's empty glass with his fingernail.

'More?'

'Don't interrupt! I can't see Nunn mustering up enough energy to kill anybody. So I leave you with Bilbow and Harry's paramour.'

'Paramour, did you say? According to Rose Coggins they were merely good friends, and he used her room for a little secret drinking.'

The red-rimmed eyes in the death's head fixed him grimly.

'Oho! And you call yourself a famous detective! You are very naïve, Chief Superintendent. Of course, the Coggins woman told you that. They all do. She's posing as a saint. Harry's friend and comforter.'

She thumped her stick hard on the parquet floor and some of the topers standing round the bar jumped and cast fearful glassy eyes in her direction.

'It was an adulterous association. I know. You're not trying to tell me that a full-blooded man like Harry, domestically celibate, was visiting a barmaid in secret just to drink stout!'

'So you know about the stout?'

'Of course I do. I know it all. Nunn and Bilbow covered the ground that you are making such heavy weather over, long ago. You should talk more with Nunn. Exert pressure on him and make him disclose more of what he knows...'

She didn't even look at Nunn. He might not have been there. And, in turn, Nunn seemed quite indifferent to what she was saying about him.

'In my opinion, Harry crumbled before temptation and gave the Coggins girl the money he got from me.'

'Why?'

'Don't ask me. When you find that out, you'll have solved the mystery. She might have blackmailed him. Or what is more likely, he might have been so infatuated with her, so grateful that she'd even look at a tumbledown wreck like him, that he gave her all he'd got.'

Two newcomers were entering the lounge. A woman, obviously from the country, dressed in her finery. Black hat with a ridiculous dummy veil draped round the crown, black coat, and mauve shoes with stiletto heels. She was followed diffidently by a man in an ill-fitting light grey suit, with a black mourning band stitched round his left sleeve. He seemed reluctant and out of place there and sheepishly removed his soft old black hat and revealed a shallow round head almost entirely bald.

Judging from the expression on Aunt Clara's face when she saw them, the hornets' nest was stirring again.

'What are Evelyn and Joe doing here...?'

Nobody seemed disposed to answer, so she replied herself.

'There's been a family row over the funeral lunch and Evelyn's walked out on them. He's buying her brandy, so it must have been a real set-to. Tell them to come over here, Nunn. But don't pay for any drinks for them. She's inherited enough from Millie's estate without that...'

Nunn didn't even draw himself up from his lolling position. He merely raised a hand and waved it at the newcomers, who pretended to be surprised at the sight of him and their aunt, picked up their drinks and made for the corner. Evelyn tottered across the polished intervening space on her spiked heels and Joe followed gingerly behind like a man on ice.

Evelyn was large, dark and plump and built like a Renoir woman but less ornamental. She had a long oval face, brown eyes and the Quill nose and mouth, one slightly snub and the other large and full-lipped. Normally, her expression was querulous and sulky; now she was smiling as though delighted and surprised to see her aunt.

Joe was nondescript. The sort you'd pass in the street without another look. He seemed smaller than his wife, although measure for measure, they were about the same height. He was the father of four grown-up and, as yet, unmarried girls, and was domineered by his five women. 'What are you two doing here?'

Joe made a gesture indicating that he didn't really know. But Evelyn was ready to explain fully, very fully.

'We've been insulted by the family. It seems to have got around that Aunt Millie's money's coming to me. That Bilbow has drunk too much and has been talkin' a lot. I've been accused of soapin' round Aunt Millie for what I could get and rejoicin' at the present murder tragedy because it's brought her money my way quicker...'

The brandy glass was still in her hand and she took a sip of its contents like a hen drinking. Joe was indulging in tonic water with a slice of lemon floating on it. The lemon embarrassed him and he put his fingers in the glass and held it firm every time he took a drink. They were, officially, Quill teetotallers and Evelyn had to explain.

'I'm upset. It brought on my spasms. Brandy is the best medicine. The doctor said...'

'Sit down and don't make excuses. Enjoy your brandy and never mind having signed the pledge. You knew I was coming here, didn't you, Evelyn? And you came to see what it was all about, didn't you? Tell the truth.'

Evelyn cleared her throat with affectation.

'We wished to pay our respects to you before you went home. We haven't seen you since Uncle Pharaoh's funeral.'

Aunt Clara turned to Littlejohn.

'Have you interviewed this pair yet? You should, you know. Evelyn was the only one of the family admitted to Great Lands and then only when Harry was absent. That's right, isn't it, Evelyn?'

Joe, still making a two-handed job of his drinking, had replaced his hat on the back of his head and sat meditating upon his slice of lemon as though he'd never seen the likes of it before.

'I used to call on my aunt whenever I could. She was lonely and helpless and Uncle Harry treated her shocking. Nothing wrong in that, was there?'

'No. It kept you in her good books, didn't it?'

Evelyn's eyes filled with tears. It must have been the brandy, for, with a stony face such as hers, tears surely came hardly.

'Don't you start picking on me, Aunt Clara. I've had enough insults from Florence to last a lifetime.'

'So, it was Florence, was it?'

'She's always the same...'

'Well, we won't discuss your drunken quarrels any further. This is Superintendent Littlejohn, who's here to find out who killed your Uncle Harry. Do *you* know?'

Joe merely shook his head dolefully, but Evelyn reared angrily.

'You aren't suggesting that we had anything to do with it, are you?'

'Had you?'

'Certainly not!'

Evelyn started to pant with emotion and her copious bosom rose as though another of her spasms was coming on.

'I don't know who did it and I can't even guess.'

'Come, now. What about Jerry?'

'You mean the police think he...?'

'I don't mean anything. Or do you think it was that woman he was keeping at the *Drovers Inn*?'

Joe's face suddenly illuminated and then the light died and left the same downtrodden expression as before. He took a cigarette from a battered packet, lit it and sat there for a minute with it dangling in his mouth. He might have been quite alone. He showed little interest in any of them. A plebeian edition of Mr. Nunn, who seemed equally bored by what was going on.

Evelyn was obviously interested in the line the conversation was taking, but trod warily as became her modesty.

'You mean she might have killed and robbed him?'

'And then carried him to his own farmyard and left his body there? I always said you were short of intelligence, Evelyn.'

'I know I was never a favourite of yours, Aunt Clara, but...'

'Did your Aunt Millie know what was going on?'

'Yes. I don't know how, but she did. She once asked me what Rosie Coggins looked like.'

'And you threw the book at your aunt?'

'No, I didn't. I just told her. She just said "Poor Harry, trailing after a girl like that, trying to keep dark what was in the wind. People must be laughing at him..."'

Littlejohn sat taking it all in. If Aunt Clara wished to do all the talking she could continue. She was better qualified in that respect than the police.

'You don't think your Aunt Millie killed Harry?'

Evelyn lost her temper with Aunt Clara for the first time. She threw discretion to the winds and turned on her.

'It's wicked of you to say such a thing. You know as well as I do that she had no strength. She moved about the house by crawling on her hands and knees. It was pitiable to see.

She wasn't capable of killing anybody if she'd wanted to. And she'd never want to. She was a saint, was Aunt Millie, and don't you be making evil suggestions about her. I won't have it.'

'All right. All right. Don't lose your temper, Evelyn. We'll change the subject. Did your aunt know that Harry had any money?'

'No. She had to keep him herself from her own little bit. It was a scandal. If he couldn't run the farm, he was fit enough to get a job and keep himself and his wife. Instead, he spent every penny he could lay hands on that woman at the *Drovers*.'

'And you were the only person who ever visited your aunt?'

'Except that Bilbow man from Mr. Nunn's office, who used to go to see her about her bits of money. He took her cash up now and then and talked what business he had to do with her. That's all... Oh, and Jerry... He sometimes went up there pretending his job made it necessary for him to inspect the state of the premises concerning vermin. He was never allowed in. Aunt Millie had no time for him and Uncle Harry chased him off whenever he saw him about...'

Aunt Clara was becoming bored with Evelyn's company and thought it time to be rid of her.

'Well, Evelyn, it's been nice seeing you, but you'd better go now. I've business to talk over with these two gentlemen and as it's private, I'd like to get on with it on our own. Good day to you both.'

The pair of them looked as if they didn't know what their next move must be, so Aunt Clara shook hands with them and they, in turn, shook hands with Littlejohn and Nunn. Then, still carrying their glasses they tottered across the polished flooring with hesitating steps and made their exit, still holding their drinks. A waiter hurried to relieve them of their burdens and they quickly drank the contents.

Joe seemed to have tried to eat the lemon in haste, for he vanished choking and holding his chest.

'Thank heaven they've gone. I never liked Evelyn. Always had ideas above her station. And Joe...'

She turned and addressed Littlejohn.

'You wouldn't think, that in his youth, Joe Bradley was the liveliest lad in the district, would you? Chasing the girls and up to all sorts of mischief. Since he married Evelyn she's reduced him to a block of wood, a sort of stooge for her gossip. Today, however... Well, I've never seen Joe looking so worried and so quiet. As a rule, he's an echo of his wife, just nodding agreement or confirming all she says. But today he might have been struck dumb. There's something in the wind. There's a lot on Joe's mind. And it's not Millie's money. You ought to talk to Joe on his own. Don't let Evelyn get anywhere near, or she'll spoil it all. When he's away from her, he'll talk like any other rational human being.'

'What does he do for a living?'

'He's a cabinet maker and a very good one, too. He works for Lovedays in the High Street. They've a workshop in the alley behind the shop. You'll find him there most days...'

She paused and wiped some flecks of foam from the corners of her lips.

'You ought to get to the bottom of what's bothering Joe... And now I'm going. I've been so busy and talked so much that I've exhausted myself. And I haven't had any food.'

She looked hard at the clock.

'It's nearly half-past two. I told Lingard to bring the car round at one-thirty. I expect he's got himself booked by the police for obstructing the square. Just go and see if he's there, Nunn.'

Nunn called a waiter and told him to do it and the man quickly returned to say that Lingard was waiting in the hall and the car was in front of the hotel annoying everybody.

'It looks as if you might have to deal with a parking matter for me in court very soon, Nunn. Help me up and then the pair of you can give me an arm apiece as I cross this silly polished floor.'

They saw her into the hall where her chauffeur, a shifty looking customer like an ex-jockey, was waiting for them. He seemed devoted to his mistress, however, and received her with a solicitous smile. She left them whilst she went in the room evasively labelled by the enterprising management *Ladies' Powder Room.*

'Wait for me. I'll need help to get in the car.'

She turned to the chauffeur.

'Go and open the door, Lingard. Don't hang about.'

She was not long away and the two men took an arm apiece again. It was then that Aunt Clara slipped a folded card in Littlejohn's hand. He quickly transferred it to his pocket. He retrieved and examined it when he'd seen the pair of them off.

It bore a message written in pencil on a visiting card in spiky handwriting.

I couldn't get rid of Nunn. I wished to tell you that we ought to discuss this matter further in private. I am available at any reasonable time at the address given here. C.B.Q.

Chapter VIII
Cromwell among the Mourners

Cromwell waited in the shadow of another large memorial covering a spacious square grave with a forgotten rose bush blooming profusely over it. He waited for the next move and it soon came in the shape of Bilbow, who seemed to be killing time until all the mourners had sorted themselves out ready to adjourn for the customary meal. Aunt Clara, Littlejohn and Nunn were receding in the distance.

'Has he left you behind to capture some local colour?'

Bilbow had been drinking. He wore a dark grey tweed suit and a black tie, both of which had seen better days. With his beard and aggressive manner he looked like a modernised replica of Captain Kettle.

'Why don't you join us for a meal? I'd be grateful if you would. You'd be congenial company for me.'

Cromwell accepted without much enthusiasm. He was thinking that there must still be money and influence somewhere in the Quill family if the funeral of a decrepit member like Harry could command the presence of Nunn and turn his chief clerk into a master of ceremonies.

'We'd better wait here until we've seen what the local newspapers call the floral tributes…'

Most of the group were studying the floral pile set out on the grass near the grave and reading aloud the remarks on the accompanying cards. Several of the throng were checking the names of the senders and seemed to have such long memories that they could detect at once those who had omitted their offerings or who were newcomers at this time. The absentees were discussed freely and much of their dirty linen was washed. One group of the Quills was concerned with who had thrown the first handful of earth on the coffins and why and when, and others were intrigued by the single red rose which had somehow appeared at the end on Harry's modest casket.

'It must have been from that woman. But how did it get there?'

'I saw Bilbow throw it on when he thought nobody was looking while the pastor was saying the prayers…'

As if, at any time, anybody could elude the careful watch of the Quills!

There was universal concern at the behaviour of Aunt Clara, who'd gone off without a word to anybody.

'She's getting senile. She was a nobody till she took up with Cousin Algy. After the carryings-on between those two before they got married, she's no cause to cast the first stone…'

There was some discussion among the more artistic Quills concerning the originality of a verse which had been written on a card attached to a wreath from Mortimer Quill, the family poet laureate, and which Cromwell remembered long after the rest of the case was forgotten.

We'll remember you, dear Harry,
And your useful life recall.

Now there's nothing left to answer
But your photo on the wall.

Except for the little corner where the black-clad Quills were holding court, the cemetery had a gay look. The trees were green and shady, the flowers on the graves were rioting with colour, the birds were singing and crowds of shouting children running about the paths gave the place an animated, almost festive air.

The gravediggers were busy filling up the double grave of Harry and his wife and one was whistling as he shovelled the earth.

The first conference adjourned, the matter of transport was next on the agenda. Some had come by bus or train; others by vehicles of all ages and sizes. The latter had now to be removed, by order, from the cemetery car park and their owners were seeking a place for them in a spot nearer the café where the feast was to be held.

It was like a rally of old crocks. Most of the Quills were either of modest means or else thrifty and ran their transport until it disintegrated. Motor bikes and sidecars, old models of now unheard-of designs and dimensions, saloons on their last legs, old vans large enough to accommodate modest quantities of livestock. Some well kept; others rusty and decrepit and splashed with cow-dung and mud. Tim Quill's new red convertible stood arrogantly among the lot.

There was an agony of rattling starters, clouds of petrol, shunting here and there and quarrelling and banging. And then they'd all gone, except Luke Quill and his exasperated wife and two daughters, whose car wouldn't start on any account and which a number of men were pushing, emptied of its vociferous women, to the edge of an incline which they hoped it would coast down to activity.

When Cromwell and Bilbow arrived at the *Good Companions Café,* most of the family were there and seated in their places. The pastor, a hungry man, had already said grace and they were waiting for someone to give the signal to fall-to. Cromwell had resisted Bilbow's persuasions to take a glass of something on the way there.

It was a second-rate place with a confusion of small tables covered with soiled plastic cloths and decorated with artificial flowers and spread with seedy cutlery. The meal was a cold one; cold meat and wet lettuce, tinned peaches with ice-cream, then coffee, and no more. Some of the mourners regretted straight away that Harry and Millie wouldn't be pleased with that kind of send-off.

Cromwell and Bilbow sat together at a table of their own in the place of honour near the podium on which longhaired guitarists performed every Saturday night. In view of family tradition, water only was available to drink and stood in thick cheap glass jugs for their refreshment. Bilbow regarded them with obvious distaste. Some of the throng, however, had called at pubs on the way there and drunk a few parting toasts to Harry and his wife. These rebels were easily identified by their behaviour, and their coarse humour and noisy talk was censured by the more discreet members of the family. Bilbow had taken more than a few drinks. He was quite talkative and Cromwell took the opportunity of asking him a few questions he'd been wanting to put since they left the cemetery.

'You're a friend of Rose Coggins?'

Bilbow chewed at his ham and lettuce contemplatively as though choosing his words.

'In a way. I've had to keep in touch on account of Harry's relationship with her...'

'Information for Mr. Nunn?'

'Yes. Why?'

'Only I heard somebody say you'd put a rose on Harry's coffin on behalf of Rose. A bit risky, wasn't it?'

Bilbow shovelled another forkful of food through his beard and spoke with his mouth full.

'She asked me to do it. She was fond of the old boy and it pleased her, though I didn't quite agree with it in view of his wife's body being in the same grave.'

'She was more than just fond of him?'

'Well... yes.'

Bilbow was in a matey, indiscreet condition of semi-intoxication and the general atmosphere of the party, with everybody being confidential at the tops of their voices, seemed to stimulate him to disclosures. After all, he and Cromwell were colleagues, strangers at the feast, representatives of the law, the police, investigations...

'The old boy's dead and buried now. The truth will do him no harm. Of late, there's been an affair going on between Harry and Rosie. They grew quite fond of one another; two lonely people so to speak. Although Harry was a queer fish for a girl like her. Still... No accounting for women's tastes is there?'

Bilbow paused in his eating to give Cromwell a sad, almost tearful look.

'No. He left her all he had, I believe.'

Bilbow savagely cut up the rest of the ham on his plate.

'He hadn't anything. Even his farm was mortgaged...'

There was a sudden uproar of unseemly laughter from a table nearby at which Tim Quill and another man, who was a stranger to Cromwell, were entertaining the two best-looking women in the room. They must have been part of the family, although they didn't in the least resemble the rest. They were both dressed with the full knowledge that mourning assumed with taste becomes a woman. They were young, lavish, good-looking and aware of it. They resisted all the efforts of the drab members of the party to repress them. Tim and his companion were enjoying themselves.

Bilbow looked at the revellers with sad appreciation.

'Tim's off the leash today and he's making the most of it.'

'What do you mean?'

Bilbow looked surprised.

'You've met his wife?'

'Yes, briefly in the course of duty.'

'I'm sure you liked her. A lady. A bit different from Tim. He's always been a woman chaser. He was bailiff for a wealthy man out Branscombe way and the daughter fell for him. She wanted him and got him. It was father's fortune that did it. The old man settled them in the finest set-up in the county.'

'It was dark when we called there.'

'A magnificent farm. Mind you, Tim's a good farmer. None better. But his wife must have regretted the day she ever set eyes on him. He settled down for a while and then broke out again. Drink, fast cars and fast women, like those two sisters he's ogling now. They're the Penderell girls from Bradfield, second cousins of Millie. They're not here for funerals, but for a good time. I bet Tim arranged for them to come. He'll give them high jinks on his wife's money, I'll say. He's left her at home, you'll notice.'

Bilbow contemplated his peaches and ice-cream and pushed them aside. Then he laughed at his thoughts.

'I'll tell you something about Tim. You'll laugh.'

He seemed to think that Cromwell hadn't shown enough interest in Tim and his adventures and was going to go one better now.

'It was Tim who introduced Harry to Rosie! You wouldn't believe it, but Tim was a good friend of Rosie for a time. His uncle had cut his hand, or something, and Tim noticed it one day at the mart. He told Harry he'd better do something about it. See a doctor. Harry said he'd no faith in doctors, so Tim persuaded him to let Rosie dress it. She'd been a sort of unqualified nurse, an orderly at a local hospital once and was quite good. Harry went in the end. And that started it. It's quite a good joke to think that tumbledown old Harry finally cut out the experienced Tim with Rosie. As I said, there's no accounting for feminine behaviour, is there?'

'And Tim resented it?'

Bilbow who was just wryly drinking his coffee, choked and spat.

'Here, here. That doesn't mean that you put Tim on the lists of suspects, you know. As you can see, he's one for taking his consolations elsewhere. Although from what I gathered, he thought a lot of Rosie and resented her relations with his uncle...'

The mourners had, even here, established themselves at the small tables according to seniority, like fowls ranged in pecking order. At the next table to their own, near the buffet, a quarrel had broken out. Two women and their husbands were occupying it; the former obviously the dominant partners, for they were now shouting and flinging their arms about to the obvious discomfiture of the men.

'I won't stay in her company a minute longer. We're going. Come, Joe, we'll finish our meal somewhere else.'

Bilbow rose and hurried across to restore order after excusing himself to Cromwell.

'Got to keep the peace. That's Evelyn, Millie's niece and legatee, who's doing all the shouting. Whenever she goes to a family party, there's a row.'

Evelyn clutched at Bilbow like somebody drowning scrambling aboard a life-raft. Both women were on their feet. The other one, a thin, stringy, bilious-complexioned peasant type, with a goitre, wore an awful black straw hat which had obviously seen half a century of funerals.

'Florence has accused me of being at Great Lands when Harry died! Which is as good as saying that I'm the murderer or I know who did it. Tell her, tell her, Mr. Bilbow, that I was there till two o'clock on that day and that you arrived there, too, and gave me a lift back in your taxi to Marcroft for my bus. I wasn't within ten miles of Great Lands that night... And Harry was killed in the night...'

She paused and put on an act of gasping for breath, to which her husband and most of the rest of the audience had grown accustomed years ago and paid no attention at all.

Bilbow was taken aback. So was Cromwell. Here was something the police didn't know.

'Harry wasn't there when we were there, was he, Mr. Bilbow? We couldn't have seen him murdered.'

Bilbow tapped her comfortably on the shoulder.

'Of course we were there together, Mrs. Bradley, and I did give you a lift. Harry wasn't at home. Neither of us saw him. Besides, the doctors say he died during the night. You've nothing to worry about.'

He stood there, swaying gently, waiting for the uproar to subside. But it didn't. Evelyn had the centre of the stage and all eyes were on her. She wasn't giving up. Without another word to the lawyer, she gathered up her large handbag and her embarrassed husband and made a spectacular exit, in the course of which she knocked over the water jug on their table and flooded her antagonist's lap with its contents.

At the door she turned back and denounced the whole family.

'I won't stay another minute with such a lot of trouble-makers. It's always the same.'

Joe shambled after her, red and out of countenance, yet smiling at friends here and there in his own shy way, assuring them that it was none of his doing and would soon blow over. As he passed the last table near the door, he paused and shook hands all round with the occupants.

A silence and then the meal went on. The conversation, stimulated by Evelyn's contretemps, grew much more animated. Some of it was spiteful, but among the more cheerful and charitable members of the family, reminiscences of happy days with those they remembered with affection, were exchanged. And then the victuals ran out and the diluted coffee all vanished and one by one, the mourners left in little knots either for home or to adjourn elsewhere for fuller more secret conferences. Tim and his boon companion left in roaring spirits with their fast young women, presumably for a spree in Tim's fast car.

Cromwell and Bilbow were left alone with the four bedraggled waitresses, whom Bilbow tipped and who then left them. The remnants of the feast littered the shabby tables over which hung the decorations and loud-speakers which enlivened the place every Saturday night. Someone had left a pair of black gloves behind and there was a woman's umbrella looped over the back of a chair.

Cromwell gave Bilbow a cigarette.

'So you were the last at Great Lands before the crime?'

'I suppose so. I'd been taking Mrs. Quill's monthly money to her. Evelyn was there with her when I got there. I gave her a lift back to town as she said.'

'Was it market day in Marcroft?'

'No.'

'Why was Harry in town?'

'I don't know. His wife said she didn't know either, but he'd told her he'd business there. That's all.'

'Any idea of the nature of the business?'

'Mrs. Quill added she expected he'd gone to visit Rose.'

'You told us before that she knew all about her...'

'That's right. She took it all very calmly, as a matter of course. She'd been through so much in her lifetime that I guess she was resigned to whatever came along.'

Bilbow looked as if he felt the same. He was exhausted and dishevelled with his day's efforts.

'Have you asked Rose if Harry visited her that day?'

Bilbow blinked and coughed as he swallowed the smoke of the fag-end which he seemed determined to consume to the bitter last half-inch.

'Yes. He went there to her room.'

'How long was he with her?'

'Don't ask me. I wasn't a spectator at their horrid amours. I suppose he stayed the usual time. Until the *Drovers* opened for the final session. I didn't press the point.'

'When did you ask her?'

'The day after the crime.'

'You haven't been very forthcoming, have you? You should have told us the first time we questioned you.'

'I didn't remember it till Evelyn started her hullaballoo. He was killed in the night. I assumed he'd gone home after seeing Rosie and it all happened long after we left.'

'We'll discuss that later, then, when the Chief Superintendent returns. Shall we go? The staff are anxious to clear up.'

Cromwell was bored with it all. The seedy party, the sordid room, Bilbow half-drunk and longing for more. It was depressing.

They left the place together, Bilbow descending the stairs unsteadily, one at a time. They parted at the street door, the lawyer to return to his office after a call or two to wash away the traces of the awful meal and Cromwell to the hotel to await Littlejohn.

❧ ❧ ❧

'What do you think of it all?'

They were in a corner of the lounge again in the stupid hotel, once a gracious Georgian building, now a modern upstart of a place with bars everywhere and affluent customers tippling at them. They didn't want to go to the police station, where the old routine would go on and Superintendent Taylor would ask a lot of questions which couldn't be answered and then he'd think the men from London had been wasting their time.

Taylor! They'd forgotten him in their preoccupation with Harry Quill and his motley crew of relations. Littlejohn would have to apologise when the case was finished. Would it ever finish?

The two detectives had exchanged information and now they sat side by side drinking whisky and planning the next moves.

'What do you think of it?' said Littlejohn.

Cromwell sat with his eyes half closed. At the back of his mind, superimposed, it seemed, on events going on around him, he could still see the Quills with whom he had spent the exhausting day. A shadowy lot in black, mostly of country stock. Some of them were mere peasants with crafty secretive ways, who lived lives quite alien and apart from their relatives from the towns. Even those who had left the land for easier better paid jobs in the towns still bore traces in appearance, dress and behaviour of the life they had left behind.

Cromwell only returned to the matter in hand after Littlejohn had repeated his question.

'It's a funny affair altogether. One thing I'm sure of: that we'll get no help from the Quill family. They hang together and they understand one another, in spite of the fact that they quarrel like a lot of Kilkenny cats. They're like the occupants of a foreign country, who don't grasp what we're after. Harry Quill was murdered. They'll soon forget that. They've their own affairs to attend to. The crime causes no passion for revenge among them, no eagerness to find the culprit. There's little or no money at stake to quarrel about, and money seems to be all they care about where the family's concerned. The funeral party today was just a normal gathering for an ordinary occasion. Harry might have died in his bed full of years...'

Littlejohn looked hard at Cromwell. His report on his day's work was discouraging and unusual for one of Cromwell's exuberant and humorous temperament. The family seemed to have convinced him that outside interference wasn't welcomed.

'Let's talk it over...'

Littlejohn began to outline the affair as though thinking aloud.

Harry Quill died in the night. The autopsy estimated between eight and midnight. There was no food in his stomach, which was strange, because, as a farmer he enjoyed his meals and was always ready for them. Presumably, he hadn't eaten since lunch time. There was, however, one strange detail. There was a fair amount of alcohol in his stomach; brandy, in fact.

Death had been due to a blow on the back of the head which, although it had not caused brain laceration, had resulted in arterial rupture which had brought on massive and fatal cerebral haemorrhage. No other traces of violence, except a minor bruise (of little consequence) on the forehead.

The initial stages of the case had been confused by erroneously associating it with the black gang farm robbers. The death blow had not been given the importance it deserved.

From information received, it appeared that Quill had left home in the morning of the day of the crime and presumably visited his mistress in Marcroft. He had travelled, as usual, on his tractor, which was found in a shed in the farmyard.

'We don't know how long he stayed with Rose Coggins or where he went after he left her, until his body was found by his wife who raised the alarm and then had a stroke from which she never recovered nor even spoke.

'Who could have been interested in Harry's death?'

Littlejohn lit his pipe and looked around him.

The place was full and both bars were working at top speed. An animated crowd of visitors occupied the lounge, laughing, talking, arguing, showing-off. A man in a turban was carrying on a lively discussion with a group of young men who looked like students. As Cromwell had said, quite another world from that of the Quills.

'Who could have been interested in Harry's death?'

His wife? She had suffered extremely from his way of life, his shiftless ways and lack of responsibility. He was living on her money and she knew he was keeping a mistress. As long as he lived, she was immobilised in their tumbledown farm, whereas, if he were out of the way, she might settle for the rest of her life in some home suitable for invalids such as she was. But, it seemed, she was far too weak to take heroic measures to rid herself of the man, too feeble to despatch him with a single blow.

Rosie? And kill the goose that laid the golden eggs? Harry, in spite of his apparent poverty, had raised money on mortgage on his ruined property. Enough to keep Rosie in comfort for a while. According to Bilbow, however, she loved Harry, strange as it seemed. Had he threatened to break it off? Had he tired of it all, as he'd tired of his farm, his existence, his family? He'd left Rosie all he had. Did she know he'd nothing to leave?

The family? Jerry and Tim? They'd both alibis, for what they were worth. Their statements had been checked and their friends had confirmed that they were both far away from Great Lands between eight and midnight on the night of the murder. In any event, the drunken shambling Jerry was no murderer. Tim, however, might have had a motive. He'd been Rosie's lover before Harry. He'd actually introduced Harry to her and Harry had ousted him from her affections. However, from all accounts, Tim found it easy to seek consolation elsewhere...

Littlejohn paused and they both sat back and ordered some more drinks. They sat there, not thinking deeply, watching the panorama of the hotel lounge unfolding itself. There was a poster on the wall opposite.

Farmers' Ball Town Hall. Grand Tombola. Dancing to the Roosters

Two men on the next seat discussing working conditions at a local factory.

'We'll tell him what we want and if he turns it down we'll bring the whole bloody lot out...'

And a man who appeared to be waiting nervously for someone. He kept crossing and uncrossing his legs and was drinking double brandies. He pretended now and then to be reading the evening paper, the banner headlines of which could be seen all over the room.

Mayor of Marcroft says to Hell with the Ministry

Suddenly Littlejohn awoke from his torpor and looked at his watch.

'Seven o'clock. We've still time for another talk with Rose Coggins.'

'Is it urgent?'

'Yes. We want to know what Harry was doing during his visit to Marcroft on the day he died. Has it struck you that he might not have been murdered at Great Lands at all? He might have been killed elsewhere and his body brought and dumped on his own doorstep later. He died after eight o'clock, but the blow which caused the fatal brain haemorrhage might have been delivered hours before. Let's go.'

On the way out they passed Tim Quill. He didn't see them. He was too occupied with the two flashy girls he'd picked up at the *Good Companions*. They might have been guests at a wedding instead of the funeral of a murdered man.

Chapter IX
Quill's Last Day

'What do you want?'

The *Drovers Inn* wasn't very active. It had been market day in the town, they had been busy in the morning and afternoon, but now there was a lull.

Rose Coggins was drying glasses and keeping an eye on her clients at the bar and seated at the tables scattered around. Four men were playing darts and another was lying asleep with his head on his arms. Rose was surprised and upset when she saw Littlejohn and Cromwell.

Criggan, the landlord, was behind the bar as well, a middle-aged, slim, hollow-cheeked man with dark roving eyes and a small moustache smeared across his upper lip. He eyed the newcomers unpleasantly. He didn't give them a chance to cause any fuss; he recognised them right away as police and hurried to meet them almost before they were through the door. He spoke quietly out of one corner of his mouth.

'What do you want?'

'To speak to Mrs. Coggins.'

'Come in here.'

He led them in a small room on the right, a cubbyhole partly used as an office and partly as a snug to be turned to public use when they were busy and overcrowded. There was an old desk there and a stock of full bottles of whisky and gin in one corner. Some small steel-framed chairs were stacked against one wall.

There was nobody there, except an elderly grey-moustached little man with a bald head. He was drinking beer and looking blankly ahead, lost in thought.

'Could you take your beer to the bar, dad?' The old man took up his glass and tottered out, still looking blankly about.

'That's my father. He's very old and he's losing his memory...'

Left to themselves, they found Mr. Criggan inclined to be a bit awkward.

'You might have chosen a better time. It's gettin' late and we'll soon be full of customers again. Rose is busy till closing time. Won't it do in the morning?'

'This is important. We must speak with her. It won't take long.'

'It all depends on what you mean by "long". I know what the police are once they get their teeth in anything. Is it about Harry Quill?'

'Yes.'

'I suppose it's no use asking what it's all about. I'll be glad when it's all settled. It's upsettin' Rose. Makin' her a nervous wreck. She's not the same girl. Her work's sufferin'. In a job like hers, you've got to be bright and cheerful and please the customers. They don't want a long face behind the bar, though many of them sympathise with her, you know. You'd be surprised.'

He looked earnestly in their faces for sympathy and found none.

'I'll take over. You can see her here. But don't be long.'

Rose arrived hesitantly. Littlejohn had never seen her so pale. All the bloom had vanished from her cheeks. There were dark rings round her eyes which made them appear larger.

'Good evening, Rose.'

She opened her mouth, but speech didn't come. She looked first at one of them and then at the other, as though she hadn't expected to find the pair of them.

'What do you want to see me about?' she said at length.

She seemed ready to turn and run.

'Come in Rose, and sit down. We don't want to upset you. We've some more questions to ask you, though. We need your help again.'

Cromwell brought her one of the silly little steel-framed chairs from the corner. There were no others except the swivel chair in front of the battered desk, which was on its last legs. The steel chairs were too small for all of them and seemed to become invisible when they sat on them. The scene was a bit comic, as they looked to be suspended in mid-air without support.

Rose sat down limply. She seemed to be lost for something to say.

'You shouldn't have come here in my working hours. It creates a bad impression and Mr. Criggan's not too pleased about it.'

'I'm sorry, but this is important. You didn't tell us everything you knew last time we were here, Rose, and a lot of what you did say was half untrue, wasn't it?'

She had no resistance left in her, by the looks of her, and she took the rebuke mildly and bit her lip.

It was obvious she was desperately worried, and had been since they saw her last. She passed her hand across her forehead in a dazed sort of way.

'Have you come to arrest me?'

'Whatever for? You've committed no crime, have you?'

'No. All I did was to try to say nothing that would smear Harry's good name. I was fond of him. He was always a good friend to me. He treated me like a lady instead of a barmaid.'

'He was more than a friend, wasn't he?'

Somehow, Littlejohn couldn't bring himself to ask if Harry had been Rosie's lover. The expression seemed farcical and out of place when used about Harry, the Don Juan with the naïve ways, old suit, cloth cap and shirt without a collar and the brass head of a stud glinting in the neckband.

'You seem to have found out all about us. Well, I'll tell you this...'

She raised her head and looked Littlejohn full in the face with some of her former confidence and energy.

'I'll tell you this: we'd have been married if circumstances had been different for Harry.'

'We'll not discuss your personal relations, Rose. We'll take those for granted. What I want to know is did Harry Quill call at your home on the day he died?'

She seemed relieved at the commonplace question.

'Yes. Why?'

'What time?'

'I found him there when I got home at about two o'clock.'

'How long had he been there?'

'About two hours, he said. He used to go to my room and wait for me if I was working. He had a key. He'd made himself comfortable in an armchair and was reading the morning paper with his shoes off. He liked being comfortable.'

Littlejohn could imagine it. Quite in keeping with Harry.

'Was he drinking stout?'

Littlejohn had to ask it to complete the picture.

'Yes. Why?'

He had known the answer before it came. He slowly filled and lit his pipe as they talked.

'What time did he leave?'

'I made him a meal. He'd some ham and pickles...'

Yes; just as expected.

'And then some cheese?'

She looked surprised.

'That's right. It sounds as if somebody saw us having our meal. Did they?'

Littlejohn felt he'd known Harry Quill and his ways and tastes for years.

'When did he leave?'

'About half-past two. He said he'd some calls to make and that he'd come back on his way home. But he never did. That was the last I saw of him, disappearing down the stairs with his broad smile on his face.'

She didn't shed a tear or create any emotional fuss. She just said it calmly, too beaten and confused even to weep.

'What was the business? Did he tell you?'

'Not exactly.'

'But you had an idea?'

She looked here and there wearily. Anywhere but straight at Littlejohn now. She was wondering how much to tell him.

'You'd better tell us all you know this time, Rose. The half-truths you told us last time we saw you have caused us a lot of trouble.'

'I didn't mean them to...'

'It will be in your best interests to be candid. You can trust us to be discreet.'

She hesitated no longer. It came out with a rush.

'He said he was going out to raise some money for an idea he had about buying a business for me.'

'A business?'

'He'd got jealous about me being in the bar. He said it wasn't right I had to put up with the coarse talk and advances of the type of men who came to the *Drovers*.'

The very thought of it seemed to put a little life back in Rosie. Her colour returned and she smiled to herself as though proud of what she'd told them. And then somebody had come along and cut Harry's idyll short.

'And he was going to get you to leave here and enter into some sort of business of your own?'

'Yes. He'd been hinting at something of the kind for some time, but I was surprised when he talked about making it real. I thought it was just a dream he had. But I'm sure he'd made some arrangements or was going to see somebody about the money. I told him he mustn't think of it. I knew how short of money he was. I had some money of my own. Four thousand pounds from Jack's compensation. I said I'd put that in, too. Harry blew up. He said I'd do nothing of the kind. He'd be angry if I touched my nest-egg. He said I'd need that some day. He insisted and when he'd made up his mind, Harry was hard to persuade against it.'

'What sort of business had he in mind?'

'A shop, he used to say. Not in Marcroft. Somewhere not far away, though, where I could start afresh and he could still come and see me.'

'A bit risky, wasn't it? You'd have been better where you were... at the *Drovers*, wouldn't you?'

'But I told you, didn't I, that he got jealous of me being here? He didn't like the types of men I had to deal with. Not that I couldn't take care of myself... But when I told him that, he got annoyed. I didn't want to upset him. Besides...'

She paused.

'Yes?'

'Once, when we were discussing it, he said he'd like to think I would be all right if anything happened to him.'

'Did he expect something to happen?'

'I don't think so. Not a thing like this; not being murdered...'

She clenched her teeth in an effort to control herself.

'No,' she said at length, 'No. He was a good bit older than me, you see. I expect that was it?'

'What sort of a shop?'

'He said I could choose, but it would have to be one that would make me a good living. He had some ideas like a sweets and tobacco shop, or a baby linen place. I said a little village store and post office would be my idea. Not that I thought we were seriously discussing it. I thought we were just playing a game. The idea that he had enough money to make it real never entered my mind. I just humoured him by playing at it.'

'And you found he really meant it?'

'Yes. A week or so before he died, he said he could lay his hands on the money to buy the business he'd been talking about. He was full of it. More excited than I ever saw him. I didn't ask him how much money. It didn't seem right. Besides, he wasn't much of a business man. Money to him didn't seem to mean very much. Until he told me about being able to get the cash to buy the shop, I though he had hardly any at all. He'd lost it all on his farm.'

'Did he ever talk to you about his farming business?'

'Sometimes. What about it?'

'Did he ever say how he got in such a wretched financial state and why he let his farm go to ruin?'

'Yes. He told me all that. It seemed to relieve him to talk about his troubles, past and present. He'd nobody else to confide in, it seemed. He'd never lived anywhere else than at Great Lands. He was born there and worked there for his father until the old man died. He married his cousin and they still lived on there with his parents. His father fooled away his money speculating and had to sell some of the land of the farm. When the father died he left Great Lands, or what was left of it, to Harry, who had to keep his mother till she died. There was no money left when the old man died. The farm had been neglected and Harry had to sweat to earn enough to maintain him and his wife and his mother. All the same, he said he was determined to buy back the lands his father sold. He said he regarded it as a blot on the family selling that land. He saved enough to buy it back in the end...'

It was what the police already knew. Old history that didn't seem to be much help.

'And, in buying it back, he broke himself,' added Littlejohn. 'He'd no money with which to work the farm.'

'Harry told me that his wife had some money of her own, inherited from a relative. He'd depended on her to invest it in the farm. But she told him straight, not a penny would she put in Great Lands. She said she'd had enough of Harry's financial disasters, that she'd thought him mad buying back the fields, and he could find his own capital to run the place.'

She paused.

'Harry said that from that day... to use his own words... he threw in the towel. All the time his father lived and Harry worked for him, the old man never paid him a proper wage. He kept Harry and his wife along with Harry's mother and himself; they were boarders, so to speak, and that counted as wages. What he paid Harry after that was mere spending-money, a pittance. He couldn't save on it. Then, when the farm became his, he'd still his mother to keep and take her interference in the farm affairs. When, at last, his dream came true, and he got back the land his father had sold, his wife wouldn't help him. Harry just gave up. He kept a few sheep and an odd cow, but he said he never wanted to turn a single sod of the land over for cultivation or pasture. He was just worn out, exhausted with working and failing, and he'd lost heart altogether...'

There was nothing new in that, either, except that it explained Harry Quill's change of mind, his transformation from a working farmer to a mere layabout, an idler, scratching up just enough to keep him alive. Then, he'd met Rosie, grown fond of her, had an affair with her and grown ambitious on her behalf...

'After all he'd told me, I was surprised when he talked of finding the money for me to start a new life. He didn't say where it was coming from. He said he'd tell me when he'd got it. He didn't want to disappoint us both. But the last time I saw him, he talked with confidence about getting it. I felt sure he'd had some luck and with his wife having money of her own, I felt I could fall in with his plan without having it on my conscience.'

'How much money did he hope to get?'

'He never said until just as he was leaving, he did mention an amount. I think it just slipped out in the excitement. He said again, had I thought about what kind of a shop I'd like. I said that depended on what it would cost. You see, you have to think about how much stock you need to make a business pay...'

It was evident that Rose was more financially shrewd than Harry Quill had been.

'And he said he could lay his hands on around two thousand pounds...'

The amount he planned to raise by granting Aunt Clara a mortgage on his farm!

'Again, he didn't say where it was coming from?'

'No. And I didn't ask him. I was determined to ask him, however, before he laid it out in a business for me. He might have been using his wife's money and I couldn't stand for that.'

'And he left you at half past two to go for his money?'

'That's what I thought.'

'I see. Did anybody else know about this?'

She hesitated now.

'This is most important. If you told anyone else, you must tell me who it was. Did you tell Harry's nephew, Tim?'

She flared up suddenly. After her subdued manner hitherto, it took Littlejohn aback for a minute.

'Why should I tell Tim Quill? He had nothing to do with it. You have no right to bring him into the conversation.'

'But wasn't your statement, made when first we called to see you, a little incorrect when you said you noticed Harry Quill's damaged hand and yourself suggested you'd dress it for him?'

'That's of no importance, as far as I can see.'

All the life seemed to drain out of Rose again and she stared at Littlejohn white and strained.

'You might think it of no importance, but when someone being interviewed by the police doesn't tell a true story and is discovered embroidering the tale to suit her own purposes, we don't trust the information she gives us. Harry Quill was introduced to you by his nephew, Tim, wasn't he?'

'I don't see that it matters how Harry and I met.'

'And Harry ousted Tim from your affections.'

'That's not true.'

'I had it on good authority. You'd had an affair with Tim, hadn't you? He was very fond of you... Don't interrupt, Rose. Hear me out and then I'll hear what you have to say...'

There was a knock on the door, or rather it was a series of aggressive bumps and the hollow face of Mr. Criggan appeared round it.

'Hey! How much longer is this going on? The bar's full and me and the wife are pulled out of the place. You'd better adjourn till tomorrow. We've had enough bother through Rose and her private affairs without having to turn customers away.'

Cromwell gently took Mr. Criggan by the arm, turned him round, gave him a gentle push and closed the door.

'Now look what you've done. It's enough to get me the sack. I'd better be getting back to work.'

'Not yet, Rose. Not until you've answered a few more questions. And if Mr. Criggan gets awkward, tell him you're assisting the police. If he tries to sack you, refer him to me. Now, Tim Quill had also been your lover in the past?'

'I suppose I must tell the truth, or else you'll be arresting me. Somebody has been trying to ruin my reputation, though, and I resent that. Tim was very good to me after my husband died. There was an inquest and he helped me with that, paid for a lawyer and, as Jack had little money and wasn't insured, Tim helped me along there, too. Then there was the matter of compensation which the insurance company tried to avoid. Tim saw that fair play was got for me there, too...'

Knowing Tim, Littlejohn could imagine, perhaps uncharitably, how he would enjoy the intimacy and help he could give to this good-looking susceptible woman.

'... We became friends and it developed into something else. I swear to you those two were the only lovers I ever took and then it was in peculiar circumstances.'

Peculiar circumstances indeed!

Tim seemed to have taken full advantage of the emotional and tragic upheaval in Rosie's life, and Harry... Well, according to all accounts, he'd begun by calling to drink stout secretly, and ended with a full-blown, almost comic love affair, started to borrow money and throw it about on Rosie and then, probably arising from his indiscretions, got himself murdered.

Tim, the well-dressed sophisticated philanderer, with plenty of his wife's money to spend, had, of all people, been ousted from Rosie's affections by his Uncle Harry. Of all the ridiculous situations!

'Harry was kind and considerate, even if he was rough and ready; Tim was cruel and possessive and was for ever reminding me what he'd done for me. I got tired of it. He was very fond of me for a while. But I wasn't the first and I knew from what I heard that I wouldn't be the last. He soon got over his affair with me. He's already had two or three others since.'

'Did you have a final row with him?'

'Yes. It wasn't losing me, I'm sure, that caused it; it was his pride.'

As well it might be! The idea of his uncle showing him to the door must have been a bitter pill.

'What did he say when you quarrelled?'

'Quite a lot. He blackened his uncle's character, laughed at his age, scoffed at his appearance. He was all the more angry because he'd heard about Harry's visits here from a friend, who said everybody knew and treated it as a huge joke against Tim. He said in the end, neither me nor his uncle had heard the last of it. He'd get his own back on Harry. "He's nearly in the gutter already," he shouted, "and I'll see he's right in it before I've done with him." I wouldn't take that too seriously, though. It's all over and forgotten now.'

'Who do you think killed Harry Quill?'

'I don't know. I don't want to know either. Harry's dead and that's an end to it.'

'Do you know Harry made a will in your favour?'

She didn't seem to care whether he had or he hadn't.

'He told me he'd done it. I said he mustn't and begged him to burn or alter it. I don't know if he did. He laughed at the time and said he'd nothing to leave me. And then he stopped and said "But I might one day be able to do something for you while I'm alive." That, I suppose was when the thought of buying me a shop came to him. Well, I don't hold it against him that I'm getting nothing. It's all for the best; there'll be no scandal if there's no will or money for me. It just showed how much Harry thought of me and I love his memory for it.'

Still no weeping and still no fuss. She might have been discussing someone still alive.

'I'd better be getting along. It'll be closing time soon and Mr. Criggan will be furious. He's been very patient and kind about it all. I don't want to impose on his kindness.'

'One more question...'

Cromwell was still sitting on his ridiculous little chair and nodding off to sleep, or that was what it looked like. Littlejohn felt the same himself. The little room was hot and airless and the questions and answers had grown formal and almost useless. From what they already knew, they could have answered them without much help from Rose.

'... You said you told someone about Harry Quill's suggestion that he might buy you a business.'

She took him up right away.

'I said nothing of the kind.'

'You implied it, though. You must tell me whom you told. It's very important.'

'I didn't wish Harry to go spending all that money on something which might prove a flop. He wasn't a business man, as his failure on the farm showed. Also, if he was finding all that capital, I wanted to make a success of it. Harry had saddled himself with a big farm and then hadn't enough left to work it properly. I didn't want to do the same if he spent money on me. I'd rather have let the matter drop at once.'

'Very sensible of you.'

'There's another thing. It was all right talking about shops, tobacco, haberdashery, stores and post offices, but what did they cost? Would the money run to that? And, if it did, how and where would we find a suitable one and were there any available at that price?'

She ought to have known Harry Quill before he started buying land and planning his huge farm which came to nothing but ruin. She was the business brain of the pair of them and didn't seem to miss a point.

'So you asked a friend for advice?'

'Yes. I wasn't going behind Harry's back, but I know if I'd suggested asking anybody's advice, he'd have resented it. He'd have asked me if I didn't trust him in the business matter. I went to see Mr. Bilbow, of Nunn's the lawyers. He comes here for a drink sometimes and besides, he looked well after me and my interests when Tim got him to represent me about Jack's death. I called to see him and put the matter before him.'

'What did he say?'

Cromwell and Littlejohn were wide awake now. Here, was something fresh, something exciting at last.

'He listened to all I said and then asked me to leave it with him.'

'When did you go to see him?'

'As soon as Harry had left. I was due back at the *Drovers* but I asked Mr. Criggan to let me off for half an hour. You see, the way Harry had talked, he was coming back to see me on his way home. He behaved as though he'd have the money with him when he got back.'

'Where from?'

'I don't know. I've said so. He didn't tell me where he was getting it and I didn't ask. It would have been taking a liberty.'

'Did you see Harry about the town as you went to Nunn's office?'

'No. He was nowhere about.'

'He wasn't in Nunn's office?'

'What would he be doing there? I'm sure he wouldn't go to see them about the legal side without telling me and discussing with me what sort of business we'd buy. No; he wasn't in Nunn's. I'd to sit in the waiting-room there for ten minutes till Mr. Bilbow was free. A young lady I didn't know came out of Mr. Bilbow's room and I saw Mr. Nunn going out as I went in. He spoke to me. I'm sure Harry wasn't there.'

'And Bilbow told you to leave it with him. You were in a hurry, though. What did you say?'

'I said it was very urgent. To make it appear so, I said I'd had an offer of a sweets and tobacco shop and the seller was in a big hurry and had others wanting to buy it. He seemed a bit put-out and advised me not to jump at anything, but to wait. There were other businesses coming in the market every day and he would do his best to find me one ...'

'Wait a minute, Rose. Let's get all this in proper order. You called to see Bilbow. Now think quietly. What did you say and what were his replies? Right?'

And he sent Cromwell to the bar to make peace with Criggan so that Rose would have no distractions.

'I said, as I told you, I wanted his advice about buying a business, as I felt I'd like a change from my present job. And then, he suddenly faced me with a thing I'd forgotten. He knew I'd got four thousand pounds compensation for Jack. He'd arranged it after Tim asked Nunn's to handle it. He said was I thinking of spending that on buying the business. I didn't know what to say.

'I did some quick thinking. I'd put it all in the savings bank at six months' notice on Mr. Bilbow's recommendation at the time. I said I wanted to spend two thousand on the business, would give notice right away, and meanwhile, a friend would lend me the money. He looked hard at me and then said I wouldn't get much in the way of what I wanted for two thousand pounds. However, perhaps the idea of a little village store with a post office would be best. I'd get a small salary for running the post office and perhaps Nunn's firm could arrange a loan for me for what it would cost to buy the store above two thousand pounds.'

'He suddenly chose the post office, did he?'

'Yes. It seemed to come to his mind very quickly. He's a smart man in spite of his drinking habits. He even said he thought he knew the very place for me. He'd let me know next morning. I thought I'd be able to persuade Harry to wait till then. If necessary I'd tell him I'd asked Mr. Bilbow about businesses; not for advice, but if they had any on their books what would suit us.'

'And that was all?'

'Yes. Having said that, Mr. Bilbow seemed anxious to get rid of me. He said he'd another client and he'd kept him waiting whilst he saw me. He'd better let me go and get on with his next interview.'

'Thank you, Rose. I think that will be all. I'm sorry this has taken so long. You've been a great help.'

'You do think Harry's two thousand was an honest deal. I'm sure he wouldn't do anything improper.'

'So do I, Rose. We'll soon find out what it was all about.'

Outside, Littlejohn found Mr. Criggan in quite an amiable mood. He even told Rose she could put on her things and go home now. He and his wife would manage. Cromwell had been applying his skilled technique of buttering-up his adversary and Criggan felt good.

On the way back to the hotel, Littlejohn told Cromwell about the Bilbow interview with Rose, details of which he'd missed.

'It seems to me that Bilbow smelled a rat about the two thousand pounds. Rose is a bit naïve and must have given her secret away without saying much. It's obvious, when she mentioned borrowing the money from a friend until she could get her own money from the savings bank, that Bilbow thought of Harry. Harry who, through Nunn, was negotiating a loan, in cash, from his Aunt Clara. Harry, who was Rosie's best friend.'

'You think Bilbow killed Harry to get the cash?'

'We mustn't jump to conclusions yet, old chap. There are other matters to see to before we can even begin to suspect Bilbow. After Rose had told him her tale, she said he seemed eager to get rid of her. To bring the interview to an end, he even said her best bet was a country store and post office, explained that she'd get a salary as postmistress, and then bundled her out.'

'What was his hurry?'

'Perhaps he wanted to be after Harry, or to tell Aunt Clara what Harry proposed to do with her money; give it all to his mistress! He was in such a hurry that he made a big mistake or gravely misled Rosie to get rid of her. Postmasters and postmistresses of large or even small village offices are most rigorously vetted before they're appointed. Bilbow knows as well as you and I do, that a woman who's previously been a barmaid wouldn't stand a ghost of a chance of getting the job. He told her the first thing that came in his head to get rid of her after he guessed what was happening to Aunt Clara's money.'

'What now?'

'We'll deal with Bilbow in the morning.'

Chapter X
Treasure Hunt

'So you think Bilbow was responsible for the death of Harry Quill?'

Littlejohn felt that to report to Superintendent Taylor, of the County police at Marcroft, was now his first duty. Not that he had neglected the local man; since the discovery that the death of Harry Quill had nothing whatever to do with the black gang, the investigation had taken a totally different aspect. In two days there had been revealed sufficient new evidence to turn suspicion in a fresh and more definite direction. Besides, the need for local routine work was arising. The Scotland Yard men would require the help of the local police.

Taylor listened patiently to Littlejohn's review of all the work he and Cromwell had done. Rosie, the Quill family, the funeral, the sifting of information and, finally, the emergence of Bilbow from it all. Bilbow, the skilled lawyer on whom Nunn, his master, depended; the adviser, legal *vade mecum* and general factotum of the Quill family; and the investigator and watchdog of Aunt Clara Quill.

'You think Bilbow did it?'

'The case is entirely circumstantial, Taylor. We'll need a lot more information before we are even justified in suspecting him. Our search for it will have to be a discreet one. If we let Bilbow know we're on his trail, we'll have a devil of a job to nail him; he's used to lawyers' briefs and evidence. Scare him and he'll wriggle out of the net.'

'What do you want us to do?'

'The first job is to complete the schedule of Harry Quill's comings and goings on the day of his death. He left home around eleven, drove to Marcroft on his tractor, as usual, and arrived here about noon. He appears to have gone to Rose Coggins's place and stayed there until she got home for lunch at two o'clock. He lunched with her and left her at two-thirty. There our schedule ends. Nobody, so far, seems to have seen him after he left Rosie's. He must have been somewhere. He couldn't have vanished into thin air.'

'He didn't go home from there, you say?'

'Rosie said he told her he was just off for the two thousands pounds with which they'd buy her business. He told her he'd call back on his way home and tell her all was well. He didn't call.'

Littlejohn lit his pipe. Taylor didn't smoke. His private office was dark and smelled of dust and old papers. He was hoping very soon now to remove himself and his men to new quarters in the Town Hall, where they'd have more light and air. It was a race between Taylor's retirement and the completion of his new headquarters.

'The next that was seen of him, as far as we know, was when he was discovered dead on his own doorstep. In my view, he didn't go home alive. He was killed somewhere else and taken and dumped at Great Lands. The autopsy put down the time of death between eight and midnight. Not, mark you, from organic damage in the brain or elsewhere, but from brain haemorrhage, arising out of a comparatively mild blow on the head. That means that although Harry

Quill perhaps died around eight o'clock at night, he might have been a long time dying from the blow. That gives us from just after half-past two in the afternoon until eight at night or later as the span in which the murder could have been committed. I may be wrong. Harry's wife might have done it. Even though she was an invalid, she might have mustered strength enough to hit him hard enough to inflict the injury which killed him. But the case hasn't pointed in Mrs. Quill's direction at all. She doesn't come out of this investigation as the type who would commit such a crime. Of course, she might have had a brainstorm and done it. In that case, Taylor, the case will end by being unsolved. Nobody knows what happened on that lonely desolate farm on the night Harry Quill died. And nobody ever will.'

'So, we try to find out whether Bilbow is innocent or guilty?'

'It's our job to do that for all parties concerned.'

'All the Quill family and all the Quill's men,' said Cromwell, who'd been calmly listening without saying anything.

Taylor gave him a deadpan look wondering if he meant it or if it was just a joke.

There was a map of the district on the wall. The room was so gloomy that a special light had been installed to illuminate it when in use. Littlejohn walked across and switched it on. Taylor and Cromwell gathered round.

'Harry Quill was murdered, either for the two thousand he'd promised Rosie he'd bring back with him, or for some other reason... let's say a crime of passion.'

Taylor made a wuff-wuffing sound which was supposed to be a laugh.

'Crime of passion? Harry Quill? That's a good one.'

He didn't know how good it might turn out to be!

'The murderer is left with a dying man and a tractor on his hands, because, as I see it, Harry Quill was unconscious and dying from the time the blow was struck until after eight that night. The criminal faces his problem of getting rid of Harry and his tractor. He decides on an ingenious solution. A gang of thieves is infesting the countryside, robbing and violent at lonely farms. Great Lands is just such a lonely place. If the murderer gets the body and the vehicle back to the farm, it will appear to be yet another escapade of the black gang. But the gang don't oblige. They get themselves laid by the heels on that very night and hundreds of miles from Great Lands. So, after all his scheming, Harry's murderer finds the police are investigating the crime with an open mind.'

'The murderer waited until after dark and then drove the trailer with the body on it, to Great Lands, dropped the body in the farmyard, parked the vehicle, and away... Is that it, Chief Superintendent?'

'Exactly. Harry wasn't going far for his money. Either to Nunn's office, or to Longton Curlieu, where Mrs. Clara Quill, who was making him the loan, lives. For the sake of argument, let's say Bilbow did it. He was hard up, needed money, and here was Harry Quill with two thousand pounds. Mrs. Clara Quill's lawyers, presumably Nunn's, had arranged the legal side of the mortgage on Great Lands which Harry was giving as security to his aunt. So Bilbow knew all about it. After Harry left her, Rosie rushed off to Bilbow for advice about how to invest in a business when the two thousand arrived. She thus let Bilbow know that Harry was off to his aunt's to collect. Rosie told us that after that, Bilbow seemed in a hurry to get rid of her. As well he might be. He wanted to be off to intercept Harry on his way back with his money. I don't know what sort of a plan Bilbow had to get hold of it. But he ended with the money, perhaps, and, what is more certain, a dying man and a tractor on his hands. He perhaps hid them until after dark and then transported both to Great Lands. Now, our problem is to find anybody who saw him doing it. There, you can help us, Taylor. Tell us what you know about the quietest ways on the map say, for a start, between Marcroft and Sprawle and Longton Curlieu and Sprawle. Then, having planned an itinerary, lend us a few men in cars to scour the area and find out if Bilbow, or anyone else for that matter, was abroad that night on a tractor.'

Taylor took a step backwards and studied the map, like an artist admiring his own, or somebody else's handiwork. He made circular gestures in front of it with his hands.

'Here's Sprawle and here's Marcroft...and this is Longton Curlieu...We'll put pins in them to indicate where they are...You see the main road from Longton Curlieu through Marcroft to Rugby passes within two miles and a half of Sprawle. If I was landed, as our murderer was, with a body and a tractor I wanted to dispose of, I'd give the main road a miss. Too busy and well-lit for secrets like that. There's what they call the Back Road from Longton Curlieu to Marcroft. The present main road's a new one that ironed out all the twists and turns of the old road. I'd go by the back road then. Longton's nine miles from Marcroft. The old road is very quiet between them; a hamlet called Bibworth and a pub called the *Toll Bar* three miles from Marcroft.'

'So, the murderer would have to go through Marcroft if he wanted to get from Longton to Sprawle...'

'That's what I was just going to point out. No. Anybody familiar with the roads round here, would know that just before you reach Marcroft from Longton, there's a turning to the right into the hills by a narrow, but good enough road to Sprawle. That's the one I'd take with my body and my tractor. Road's good, very little traffic, dark at night... The very thing. There are two small villages along it before you reach Sprawle Corner. There's Coopers Cross and Hanging Newstead. Each has a pub. The *Jolly Tinker* at Coopers Cross and the *Dick Turpin* at Hanging Newstead. Dick Turpin, by the way, was never executed at Newstead; never came within a hundred miles of it. The pub's a small one which does well with coach parties at week-ends, but quiet after dark.'

'Which gives me an idea. If Bilbow was the culprit, he'd be certain to need a drink to see him through. Quite a number of drinks, in fact. He's a real soak and a job like that would make him thirstier than ever. He'd probably call at one or all the pubs *en route* for whisky. Someone at one or another of the inns might have noticed him and his tractor. We'll try them. Cromwell, it's a nice day. We'll go ourselves to Hanging Newstead and call on the *Dick Turpin*...'

Taylor excused himself. Court day, he said. So they went without him.

They soon found the road Taylor had pointed out on his map. It rose into the hills, steeply in some parts, to join a secondary highway which seemed to originate in the direction of Longton Curlieu and travel to Rugby, via Poynton Harcourt, as the sign posts had it.

They went through Coopers Cross and stopped for a drink at the *Jolly Tinker*. The pub had also been a farm once and was occupied by a man and his wife, who looked like tinkers who had settled down, and their many children. The place had a beer licence only and although Littlejohn and Cromwell tried out their drink and found it quite good, they couldn't imagine Bilbow wasting much of his time at a place which didn't sell whisky or other spirits of some kind.

Mr. Houlighan, the landlord, was anything but jolly and denied ever having seen anybody like Bilbow or heard a man driving a tractor in the dead of night. He wanted to know what it was all about and what the pair of them were doing there at all. He suggested that they should go about their business and let him get on with his. He was a big man with a cauliflower ear and might have been a boxer in his time. He began to make pugnacious gestures as the gingerly interview progressed and, as Littlejohn and Cromwell were too busy to stimulate him to a free-for-all, they bade him good day and left him still talking to himself. Later, Taylor explained that the man had recently appeared in county court for debt and that presumably he mistook Littlejohn and Cromwell for bailiffs.

Chasing about among the hillside roads and quiet country places reminded Littlejohn of those treasure hunts indulged in by members of motor clubs, who ransack the neighbourhood for clues and hints as to where the ultimate triumph is to be found. According to Taylor's map, their next port of call was the *Toll Bar* on the old road between Longton and Marcroft. This involved a return to town and a trip to the hamlet of Bibworth, a small scattered group of cottages with a pub and a stone quarry adjacent.

The *Toll Bar* turned out to be a melancholy sort of place. The landlord was a little fat florid man with a worried look who recognised the police at once. His face fell and he immediately gave himself up.

'Mr. Bell?' said Littlejohn, fortified by the sign over the front door and the fact that he was licensed to sell not only beer and tobacco, but wines and spirits as well and thus satisfy Bilbow's thirst if he came that way.

'Police?' said Mr. Bell.

'Yes, sir.'

'Right. I've been expecting you for the last three years and we might as well get it over.'

He looked a bit defiant, but the way his body sagged and beads of sweat sprang all over his forehead and bald head disclosed that he was afraid as well.

'I hope you'll be able to keep my wife out if it. It was my suggestion and all my fault.'

'What are you talking about, Mr. Bell?'

'Bigamy. I ran away with my wife's sister when I found out that my brother-in-law, her husband, was carrying on with my wife. We got married to make it decent, but as we were already married, we knew we were breaking the law. We took this pub because it was out of the way, but, as they used to teach us in Sunday school, be sure your sins will find you out. We've been happy while it lasted...'

Having thus explained his confused position, he looked round the empty taproom to make sure there were no spectators and, satisfied on that point, he burst into tears.

The two detectives were flabbergasted. They'd hardly got in at the door before the whole fantastic confession was off Mr. Bell's chest.

'For heaven's sake, Mr. Bell, don't tell us any more. If you murdered your brother-in-law before you ran away, don't disclose it! We're too busy to handle another crime at present...'

'You're not here to arrest me for bigamy?'

'No.'

'Well what am I going to do and what are *you* going to do? I've confessed.'

'Forget it. Except that I'd like to give you a piece of advice. Don't go on living in sin and fear like this. See a lawyer, settle it up, and enjoy your happy existence together. Have you got a lawyer?'

'Yes. He made my will. Mr. Nunn, of Marcroft. He's a good solicitor. I'll think about what you say and likely as not, I'll see him. Do you think he'll be able to settle it all without a court case?'

'I don't know. That will depend on the circumstances.'

Mr. Bell seemed very relieved.

'Have a drink on the house.'

They had a pint of beer each.

'What can I do for you gentlemen?'

Mr. Bell looked ready for anything.

'Do you know Mr. Bilbow, Mr. Nunn's clerk?'

'Yes. It was him really that looked after my will. You see, I had to make sure that my bit of money went to Florrie and not to Prudence. Prudence was my first wife... Bilbow handled it all very well, though I didn't, of course, tell him the full story.'

'Has Bilbow called here lately?'

'He was here last Tuesday night. It was late on, too. Nine o'clock or thereabouts.'

'How did he seem?'

'As usual. He's a very even tempered, calm sort of chap, although he seems to take a good deal of whisky. He drank two doubles here and had a flask filled up with whisky. Why?'

'Just a routine enquiry. He's involved in a case we're on.'

'He'll do the job well, then. He's a good lawyer. They say he's fully qualified, but has had bad luck.'

Mr. Bell's mind was mainly employed on his own minor misdemeanour and luckily he didn't ask any more questions.

'What was he doing here at that hour?'

'He said he'd been out for a long walk and had got a bit out of his direction. He was going to take the shortest road back to town after his drink. He drank a couple and went off without any delay. It was dark, you see, and these roads are a bit tricky at night.'

'He wasn't in a car, then?'

'No. He said he was walking. I didn't go out with him. We'd a few customers at the bar and we was involved in a discussion about football. I didn't hear a car driving off. In any case ...'

Another blank! Littlejohn excused himself, saying he wished to get back to town for lunch. Mr. Bell thanked them profusely, said he'd accept Littlejohn's advice and take whatever medicine was coming to him, and saw them off.

Once out of Mr. Bell's way, they looked at the map again and by devious small roads arrived at Hanging Newstead. The *Dick Turpin* was there. You couldn't miss it. There was a hanging sign depicting a fading version of Dick, very badly set on Black Bess, jumping over what was supposed to be a fence.

The place had recently been done up, re-whitewashed and an annexe added in which they could see tables set out for anybody who cared to dine there. *Coach Parties Welcome. Free Car Park.* And the usual notice over the door announcing that John James Wilbraham was licensed to sell all that was expected of him.

It seemed quite a popular place, there were three cars and two charabancs standing in the park and in the annexe members of a Women's Institute were just sitting down to lunch after singing *Jerusalem* with great enthusiasm.

Mr. Wilbraham met Littlejohn and Cromwell at the door. He, too, recognised the police. He was a pasty-faced, youngish man with a small moustache, like two commas, ornamenting his upper lip.

'You might have chosen a better time to call. We're pulled out of the place today.'

There was a small dining-room in the main hotel, too, occupied by two or three men who looked like commercial travellers. A good-looking blonde, Mrs. Wilbraham, was rolling her eyes and generally having a good time with two of them, much to the discomfiture of her husband, who was extremely jealous of her and resented, too, her preference for entertaining male company instead of working hard at the catering.

'It's always the same,' he told Littlejohn, who didn't quite know what he was talking about, but who guessed, judging from the landlord's constant scrutiny of his wife to make sure she didn't go too far.

'What do you want?'

'I'll not take up much of your time. Do you know Nunns, the lawyers of Marcroft?'

The penny seemed to drop with Mr. Wilbraham, who had been puzzling about the purpose of their visit.

'So that's it! Mottershead has seen the lawyers about it, has he?'

Littlejohn had never heard of Mottershead or how he had suddenly become involved in the case, but he let it go.

'Yes.'

'I should just think so.'

'You know Bilbow?'

'I didn't till this turned up. The silly little devil. He thought he'd get away with it, but Mottershead saw him in the bar and twigged who'd done it. He said he'd make him pay for it.'

'I haven't heard full details.'

'I have. More than full. Benbow, or whatever his name is, called here last Tuesday night after dark... Nearly closing time, it was, getting on for ten. He was half seas over when he came in and he drank two double whiskies. Then he went out. Do you know what he was travelling in? I didn't see it myself, but it was a farm tractor. Now what was he doing with that? Had he pinched it? Is that what you're after? However, to cut a long story short, he'd put it in a dark corner of the park, and on his way out he ran into Mottershead's Jaguar. Only been new a week. Crumpled up the wing like a piece of paper. And then rushed off without stopping. A customer who was sitting in his own car with a girl saw it all and said he'd recognised Benbow.'

Here it was. All without asking.

'I'm a bit surprised that Mottershead's got onto it already. He was going for a fortnight to the South of France the day after. Luckily, he said, he was off by plane and the friend he was staying with was lending him his own car. He was going to put the matter in the hands of his lawyer before he went away and then take it up again when he came back from his holiday. I didn't know he was back yet.'

'Will you kindly give us the address of Mr. Mottershead and also that of the young fellow who saw Mr. Bilbow manoeuvring his tractor so unsuccessfully?'

'Mr. Mottershead is the owner of a carpet factory in Marcroft. Anybody'll tell you where it is. I don't know his private address. It'll be in the telephone directory.'

'And the young man in the car?'

Wilbraham rubbed his chin hesitantly.

'I don't know about him. He wouldn't thank me for getting him involved in a court case where he'd have to say he saw Bilbow damaging the car while he was canoodling with a girl in the car park, would he?'

'He won't be able to avoid it. If you don't give me his address, I think Mr. Mottershead's lawyer will find it.'

'I don't know it. It'll be in the directory, too. He's plenty of money. His father runs a betting-shop. Name's Smollett.

Bert Smollett. Don't say I put you onto him. He's married and the girl wasn't his wife.'

Cromwell made a note of the information and, as Mr. Wilbraham was showing signs of distress, owing either to Mr. Smollett's coming predicament or else to his wife's wayward behaviour with the commercial travellers, they let him go.

'This has been a lucky part of the investigation, Bob,' said Littlejohn. 'Sheer luck. Due to the fact that Bilbow just had to have a drink to keep him going, he's scattered his tracks all over the countryside. I wonder how he got home after he'd left the body and the tractor at Great Lands...'

They called at all the garages on the main road back to Marcroft, but nobody seemed to have seen Bilbow. He'd evidently not risked hiring a taxi. In any case, most of them were closed after he'd finished his gruesome job.

'He must have walked all the way back. A good ten miles. He'd be in a shocking condition when he arrived home.'

It was half past two when they got back to Marcroft and there they ate a late lunch over which they discussed their plan of action.

Cromwell was to call at Nunn's and interview Mr. Nunn himself and then Bilbow, and Littlejohn to make a trip to see Aunt Clara at Longton Curlieu.

'I promised I'd call and have a talk with her. I guess Harry Quill went there, after he'd seen Rosie, to collect his two thousand. Aunt Clara told me she'd arranged a mortgage over Great Lands and Harry had collected two thousand in cash. Now, it turns out, he *hadn't* got his cash. Aunt Clara will have some explaining to do.'

They both felt they were on the verge of important developments. It was one of those times, which occur in every case, when the end seems very near.

Chapter XI
Prosecution and Defence

Mr. Nunn was in court when Cromwell arrived at his office, but was expected at any time. When he returned, he wore the same bored, relaxed manner as though, win or lose in a case, it was all the same to him. He invited Cromwell in his room and gave him a cup of tea.

'How's the case going, Inspector? Any nearer the winning post?'

'Not yet. We're still pursuing our investigations.'

'The usual modest comment. What can I do for you?'

'It's about Mr. Bilbow...'

'Ah! What's Bilbow been up to?'

He slowly took a cigarette from a gold case and offered Cromwell one.

'He seems to be the Quill family factotum and we've realised that we don't know a thing about him. I understand he's a solicitor in his own right.'

'Correct. He was once a partner in a prosperous London firm. They parted company.'

'I think I can guess why.'

'I'm sure you can. When prominent counsel takes on a brief in a murder trial he doesn't expect the solicitor for the defence to be drunk and incapable when the case is called.'

There was a pause. Outside the sun was shining and the square was occupied by the vegetable market. It was like a scene somewhere in the South of France. The torpid, colourful atmosphere seemed to affect Mr. Nunn. He appeared more languid than ever. He stretched his long legs and put his feet on his desk.

'What exactly is this all about?'

Cromwell had to be very cautious. If Bilbow were later arrested, it was quite in the cards that Mr. Nunn would have to spring to his defence.

'Just that he's mixed up in this case through being involved with the family. When I leave you, sir, I want to have a talk with Mr. Bilbow. He dealt with, for example, a loan which Mrs. Clara Quill made to Harry Quill just before his death. He does quite a lot of work for Mrs. Quill, I hear. We don't wish him to discuss with her and any other members of the family the matters we care to question him about. I want to know what kind of man we're dealing with.'

Cromwell did not mention that Aunt Clara's story about Harry Quill having already accepted the cash for the loan from her, differed from that of Rose Coggins who said he hadn't. Littlejohn wished to challenge Aunt Clara about her version face to face.

Nunn giggled and smoothed his hair.

'So you've come to me for a testimonial?'

'I've come to make quite sure that you, as principal of this firm, approve of our questioning Mr. Bilbow about the affairs of the Quills.'

'I don't mind at all. But, I must warn you, if any of them feel they need a solicitor when or whilst you question them, they will run to Bilbow or me, and we will have to take their side. As for Bilbow... All right, question away, subject to what I've told you.'

'Is he married, by the way?'

'Yes. His wife left him years ago. It was his fault, but being Catholic she refused to divorce him. That, I understand, is what started his immoderate drinking. He's to be pitied, in a sense. He's a confirmed alcoholic who doesn't wish to be otherwise. He comes of a very good family, is a brilliant lawyer, especially in court cases, when he applies his mind to it, and he has a brother, who, under a *nom-de-guerre* is regarded as one of our top-ranking English novelists. So there you are. That's Bilbow. I don't know what I'd do without him. Has he got himself involved or incriminated in this Harry Quill affair? But, don't answer that. Go and see him and deal with him as you think fit. I don't want to be living in two camps. If Bilbow gets in trouble, I shall have to do my best to get him out of it. Bilbow's in his office. Go now.'

Nunn had suddenly assumed a very businesslike attitude. He sat straight at his desk, his languid eyes and face lively and alert and, for a brief minute, Cromwell saw the Nunn who was regarded as the best lawyer in the county. Then it was over. The hand Nunn gave him as Cromwell thanked him and said good-bye, was extended casually and slowly. The faint smile was back and the feet gently returned to the desk.

Cromwell found Bilbow in his small room at the back of the block. He looked to have been flung there along with the rest of the rubbish. He occupied a chair at a large table which might have been thrown out of the principal's room in the middle of the last century. There were deed boxes and bundles of papers along three of the walls and a new filing cabinet in which he presumably locked the more confidential documents which he handled. There were three *SPY* drawings of judges, long dead and gone, hanging askew on nails in the wall in company with a large vulgar calendar issued by a firm of local grocers.

In spite of his regular consumption of whisky, Bilbow didn't look in any way decrepit physically. He seemed of the changeless type; perhaps his beard hid the slow deterioration of all that went on beneath it. He was half-buried in a mass of documents, he was examining a tricky title and when he raised his eyes, he didn't seem a bit surprised to see Cromwell there.

'Can you spare me a few minutes?'

With this massive understatement, Cromwell entered and sat down on a hard wooden arm-chair at the other side of the desk.

'Of course. Glad to see you. What can I do for you?'

'It's about the Quill affair.'

'Still bothering you?'

'Yes.'

'Would you like a drink and then we'll talk?'

'No, thanks. I've a lot to do before I relax.'

'Mind if I do?'

He rose, removed a bottle and glass from one of the drawers of the steel cabinet, took a good drink, and then sat down again.

'Now. What's worrying you?'

He wasn't drunk, but Cromwell was sure as he looked in Bilbow's misty-blue eyes, that the man was living in a half-world where sensation was dulled and most problems swept into a kind of moral rubbish dump. He must have known that sooner or later the police would come upon his own involvement in the case and face him with it. Yet, he didn't seem in the least anxious or perturbed.

'What's worrying you?'

A different kind of set-up from Mr. Nunn's sumptuous room with its tasteful expensive contents. Here it was cold and damp. The window faced north and overlooked a yard full of packing cases and the entrance to a boiler house with a heap of coke at the door. Bilbow didn't seem to mind. He was a bygone and a failure, tucked away with the odds and ends of the partnership in which he didn't share, in spite of his reputed forensic skill. Here, in his workshop he did what he had to do to earn his pay, and then went out when he felt like it to enjoy himself at the bars of the town.

'We've been trying to compile a schedule of what Harry Quill did on his last day...'

Cromwell recited it. Leaving home, arrival at Rosie's place, departure to collect his money and then... Quill's ultimate arrival, dead, on his own doorstep.

'He left Rosie, travelling as usual, in his eccentric way, on his old farm tractor. He drove it somewhere. We think it might have been to Longton Curlieu to see his aunt, Mrs. Clara Quill. The Chief Superintendent is on his way there now to see her and enquire if he turned up there. Have you any idea where Harry Quill spent the time last Tuesday after he left Rose Coggins's place?'

Bilbow blinked and made a show of thinking hard.

'Tuesday afternoon, eh?'

'Yes. Where were you then?'

'Am I supposed to provide an alibi, Cromwell?'

'Yes. It's routine, as you well know.'

'I was, as you already know, at Great Lands until after two o'clock, returning with Evelyn to whom I gave a lift in my taxi. I returned to my office where members of the staff came in and out and I saw two clients. I can produce all of them if you insist.'

He still didn't seem in any way put out. If Cromwell thought to surprise him or intimidate him into a confession or unwary remark, he knew such tactics were of no use. Bilbow had, by his training, learned all there was to know about that technique.

'And after five o'clock, I took some work home and after having tea at a local café – they'll remember me there – I went to my flat and worked till nearly midnight. A lawsuit about land which is a bit involved. I was alone. I occupy one of a block of non-service flats and I look after myself. So, I can't verify that for you.'

'Are you sure?'

'Dead certain. Do you doubt me?'

'I don't understand that. We've been told on good authority that you were out on the back road between Longton Curlieu and Sprawle at around ten o'clock on Tuesday night. You called for drinks at two inns on the way.'

'Is that so? I must have forgotten...'

He said it as though he'd neglected to bring home the joint for the week-end or the bacon for breakfast. He got up and took another drink.

'Sure you won't?'

'No, thanks. Is that true?'

'Yes. I'd forgotten. I did take a stroll for a drink in a fresh place. I thought it would do me good after an evening's work.'

Now he was shaken. Fumbling about in his addled brain for a way out.

'A stroll did you say? I don't know the distances around here, but you must have covered more than twenty miles.'

Bilbow actually lit a cigarette and smiled broadly, baring his tobacco-stained teeth through his beard.

'I'm quite up to walking that distance when I feel inclined.'

'But you didn't. You travelled on Harry Quill's tractor.'

Bilbow pondered. He might have been making up his mind to accept or decline some offer Cromwell was proposing.

'That's right. I don't know who your witnesses are, but I guess it has something to do with an insurance claim. Am I right?'

'That does arise, but it's not the main proof. You were seen by several people.'

Bilbow nodded.

'I slipped up by risking taking a drink to cheer me on my way. Well, what about it?'

'Where did you come upon Harry Quill's tractor?'

'I'm not going to tell you that, Cromwell. I'm going to reserve my defence. I'm not obliged to give you information that concerns a client. That's a matter for the courts.'

Cromwell looked at his watch. Quarter to five. Littlejohn must be with Mrs. Clara Quill now. In fact, if their calculations were correct, he'd have enjoyed quite a little chat with Aunt Clara already.

'Hadn't we better call and consult your client then?'

'I think not. Not for the present.'

Bilbow must have had to keep sober spells whenever he had any close work or tricky cases to handle, for now, half intoxicated, he seemed to be fumbling in his mind for his next move. Finally, he decided.

'It seems to me that you are trying to find me guilty of some crime or other...'

'In the first place, for the removal of the tractor without the authority of the owner. Don't interrupt me, please. You hadn't got his authority. Harry Quill was either dead or dying when you took his tractor and drove it to Great Lands and left it in the shed. You also carried freight... dangerous freight. The dead body of Harry Quill, which you deposited on his own threshold.'

Bilbow giggled.

'By God! You've constructed a very good circumstantial case, but you can't prove it. I could soon drive a carriage and pair through that effort.'

'You'll be a wizard if you do. Don't forget, we have witnesses who saw you. Do you know that at the *Dick Turpin*, where you took your final drink and stove-in a Jaguar car in your fumblings to get out of the car park, you and the tractor were seen as plain as in daylight by a man, canoodling with a girl, sitting in an unilluminated car a few yards away?'

'I know a Q.C. who could soon demolish that. A pair of lovers, engrossed in their own passions, watching goings-on in the car park outside! The whole sorry frame-up would vanish in smoke at the hands of a skilled cross-examiner.'

'You seem to forget that you roused the whole neighbourhood when you hit a massive car such a blow that it crumpled up one of the wings like paper. But let's leave legal arguments out of it. You look like facing a more serious charge than hit-and-run in a car park.'

Bilbow took another drink and then slouched back to his seat.

'Look, Cromwell. Do you mind outlining the case for the prosecution as you've already built it up? It will be a great help to me in defending myself, if you do.'

The cheek of the man! He was treating the whole business as a theoretical exercise in law, just as though when it was over, he would stroll out and do the rounds of his bars, as usual.

'Certainly, I'll tell you. You were short of money. You always are.'

'Granted. I'm always short of money. The pittance I earn here doesn't square at all with my tastes and wishes. But I don't go and kill the first man I come upon who has a bit of money of his own. If I were desperate, I could borrow it.'

'Where?'

'I have clients who'd help me.'

'Much easier to take it when it's easy to do it.'

'In that case, I could do a smash and grab at the local jewellers. Anything rather than kill a man and spend the rest of my life in gaol if I were caught...'

'I thought I was presenting the case for the prosecution. In court, you don't have both sides shouting one another down at the same time. Will you listen? You can defend yourself after.'

'Fair enough. Carry on. I'm sorry.'

'You were short of money. You admit it. Last Tuesday afternoon Rosie Coggins called on you. She wanted advice on what she calls buying a little business. She mentioned a figure which you knew was the amount Mrs. Clara Quill had arranged to lend Harry on mortgage. You decided from what Rosie said that Harry was on his way, even then, to collect the cash from his aunt. After she'd told you that, you were in a very great hurry to dispose of Rosie. You almost pushed her into the street. You were eager to get away yourself and intercept Quill and his money. He resisted, and you struck him. He died from the blow later.'

Bilbow almost pounced on Cromwell across the table.

'Stop! You can't prove a word of that. I wanted to be rid of Rose because she was wasting my time. I'd a client waiting for me.'

'Very convenient.'

'I told Rose that, didn't she tell you?'

'You went out to Longton Curlieu and found Harry Quill there. You got your money at the expense of Quill's life. You were left with the body and the tractor. You'd a problem on your hands. Should you bury it? Or throw it in a pond?'

Bilbow laughed outright.

'I am enjoying this. You've a very fertile imagination, Cromwell. Good job you're on the right side of the law. Go on. Tell me what I did next.'

'You remembered the case which was in all the newspaper headlines. The black gang, robbing farmhouses in lonely places and not stopping at violence. You decided that would suit you very well. Harry Quill wasn't dead, however. Just unconscious. But he wouldn't recover consciousness. And then, before it grew dark enough for you to take the tremendous risk of moving him to his lonely farm, Harry died. You'd murdered him.'

'Just one word, if you please, Cromwell. That kind of forensic skill in court is quite out of date. Went out with Marshall Hall. You'd have to do better than that. Juries won't stand for illuminated and fancy appeals to their emotions. The summary court would throw that out in the street right away. I won't even defend it. It's just a lot of imaginary twaddle.'

'Twaddle or not, sir, you were seen transporting the body of Harry Quill on his own tractor from Longton Curlieu to Great Lands farm last Tuesday night...'

'Assuming that I did move the tractor, as you say, and witnesses saw me doing it, how do you know that I had the body of Quill with me? Have you witnesses of that?'

The telephone at Bilbow's elbow suddenly rang. They had been so immersed in argument that it made them both jump. Bilbow took up the instrument with a look of relief. It gave him a bit more time to think.

'It's for you. Your boss, Chief Superintendent Littlejohn.' He passed over the instrument.

'Would you like me to leave you alone with him?'

'No thanks. Stay where you are.'

Not on your life, thought Cromwell. Henceforth, he wasn't going to let the wily Bilbow out of his sight.

'I'm just ringing you from Mrs. Clara Quill's home at Longton Curlieu. Mrs. Quill has been giving me some information which will help us very much. I'd like you to come over here right away and we'll have it in writing. Is everything all right with you?'

'Yes, sir. I'll tell him and bring him with me.'

Bilbow must have wished he'd been able to listen in to the conversation. He fumbled in a drawer as Cromwell received the message, but that was an obvious blind as he strained his ears to catch what was going on.

'Good-bye, sir.'

Cromwell hung up and sat back with a sigh.

'I'm sorry, Mr. Bilbow, but that puts an end to our arguments for the time being. We'll resume later.'

'Yes. And I'm afraid when we do, I must have Mr. Nunn in with us to hear the direction the matter is taking. I didn't kill Quill, which is the way your arguments were leading. I didn't kill him and you can't prove I did.'

'That will have to wait. The Chief Superintendent wants me to go to Longton Curlieu right away. He's with Mrs. Clara Quill and she's made a statement which involves you. The Chief wants you to accompany me.'

'And if I refuse?'

'You are Mrs. Quill's lawyer, aren't you? That's a second reason why you should be there. She's going to sign the statement which concerns you. You'd better be there.'

'I don't see why. Mr. Nunn could go...'

'The Chief said *you* were the one who was required.'

'And if I say I still won't go?'

'Then I shall take you to the police station and Chief Superintendent Littlejohn and Mrs. Quill will have to join us there.'

'Take me? What right have you...?'

'Under arrest. You'll be required, for the time being, to explain what you were doing with a murdered man's tractor on the night of Tuesday last. I said, for the time being. When the Chief arrives with the statement from Mrs. Quill, it will be a more serious charge... Much more serious.'

For the first time Bilbow showed emotion. He sprang to his feet and leaned across to Cromwell in fury. Froth appeared at the corners of his mouth which he opened wide as he shouted.

'We'll see about that. So Clara has made a statement, has she? I wonder what she's said. We'll go and find out and see if it's legal and proper. Have you got a car? We're going to Longton Curlieu to find out what's been going on and if there's been any hanky-bloody-panky the police had better look out...'

And with that, all the fizz seemed to leave him. He shuffled about quietly, without saying anything more, put away all his papers and slipped on an old soiled raincoat.

'Ready?'

Before they left and he locked the last drawer of his metal filing cabinet, he found the bottle and took a good drink.

'You won't want a drink to sustain you, Cromwell,' he said as he put the bottle away and snapped the lock to. 'You're on the winning side just at present. But we'll see. We'll see.'

The market outside was just closing up and on the way across the square to Cromwell's car, a man with an almost empty stall accosted Bilbow and offered to sell him a codfish cheap. 'It's the last of the lot.'

Bilbow told him to go to hell.

Chapter XII
Trial and Error

Longton Curlieu was a small village about nine miles from Marcroft. It had remained unspoiled, perhaps because it lay about half a mile from the main road or, most probably, because it hadn't, as yet, struck any enterprising builder to develop and ruin it.

Littlejohn called at the village inn to ask the way to Longton Lodge. There were a few locals around the bar, including a man he'd seen before. It was the chauffeur, who looked like a jockey, who had driven Aunt Clara's old car at the funeral. His name was Lingard. He looked different, more dilapidated without his uniform. He wore corduroy trousers and an old coat, his grey hair was dishevelled and he hadn't had a shave.

The landlord of the *Longton Arms,* of whom Littlejohn had enquired the way, pointed to Lingard.

'He's the gardener there. He'll show you the way. He's just here for his afternoon pint, as usual. Hasn't much use for five o'clock tea.'

Lingard didn't seem amused.

'I'm not goin' back. I've done my whack for today. But I'll show you where it is.'

'Perhaps you'll have another pint with me, Mr. Lingard. It's a thirsty day.'

'I don't mind.'

There was a wooden seat outside. The weather was hot and it was quiet there and out of the way of the ears of the rest.

'Let's drink it on the seat by the door.'

The bench was usually occupied by old men in the evening and the rest of the time by walkers with their sandwiches. It was obvious the idea didn't appeal to an able-bodied, seasoned drinker like Lingard, whose natural habitat was as near the bar as he could get. All the same, as Littlejohn was paying, he was ready to satisfy his whim. He lit his burned out old pipe and shambled out.

Littlejohn ordered two pints of the beer advertised by a card on the counter. *Saint Matthew's Extra Strong Ale.* The church, visible through the trees, was dedicated to that fortunate apostle and every year the brewers made a specially strong drink for his festival.

Lingard was a bit shifty. Littlejohn had found him that way when first he'd met him. Among his own companions he was relaxed enough. His shyness with the police was perhaps because he was faced with a problem.

'I promised Mrs. Quill I'd call on her and here I am. Are you her full-time gardener?'

'Aye. Sometimes I drive the car when she wants it. I dig graves at the church, too, when they're needed. I'm one of the bell-ringers.'

He was already thawing under the strong ale, which he'd almost drunk already. Littlejohn ordered him another.

'You seem to be quite a busy man.'

'Every little helps.'

He wiped the froth of the second pint off his lips with the back of his hand.

'I saw you at the funeral. Pity about Harry Quill. Did you know him well?'

Lingard hesitated and contemplated his almost empty glass.

'Can't say I did. I seen him once or twice and just passed the time of day with him. He wasn't a reg'lar caller at the Lodge. Mrs. Quill hadn't got much time for him.'

A pause whilst they drank again. Lingard ruminated awkwardly, his large dirty hands on his knees.

'They tell me he called to see Mrs. Quill on the day he died.'

'Aye.'

'You were there, gardening?'

'Aye.'

The laconic replies were perhaps something to do with the shifty manner.

'What time did he arrive?'

The man looked at a large silver watch which he took from the side pocket of his trousers, as though it had registered the time in question.

'Mid afternoon. Around four o'clock.'

'What time did you finish that day?'

'Six o'clock. I was late. I was diggin' up the sparagrass bed. It took longer than it should have done. Couch grass in it. That's why I'm off early today. Work late one day in the week, leave early another. Mrs. Quill won't pay no overtime.'

'How did Harry Quill seem?'

'All right. Smilin' and happy, he seemed to be. Little did he think that he'd meet his Maker that night, you can be sure o' that.'

'What time did he leave?'

'I don't know. He hadn't gone when I went at six. His tractor was still there.'

'Did he arrive, as usual, then, on his tractor?'

'Yes. Mrs. Quill got wild about it. "Take that ugly thing off my front drive," she says, "an' put it in the back stables. I won't have it disfiggerin' my garden." So he had to shift it.'

'He was there when you left?'

'Aye.'

'Having his tea?'

'Not likely. Havin' a row, more like.'

'What makes you say that?'

He hesitated again.

'I shouldn't talk about what goes on at the house, but as Harry Quill's dead and past harmin', I can just say that he seemed to be there on business and Mrs. Quill didn't agree at all with what he told her. Hit him, she did. That must be on her conscience to her dying day. To have struck a man with her stick and him to die later that night. We ought to be more careful, oughtn't we? We never know what's in store for anybody and to let the sun go down on our wrath might make us regret it ever after.'

Lingard's ecclesiastical duties flavoured his conversation now and then and here he was ranting a little homily on Harry Quill. Littlejohn ordered him another drink to comfort him. 'Mrs. Quill hit Harry, did she?'

'Yes. Raised that heavy stick of hers and belted him over the head. I'd like to see her do it to me. I'd hit her back.'

'Did Harry?'

'No. He sat down hard on the first chair he could find.'

'And then?'

'I saw no more.'

'Where were you whilst all this was going on?'

'At the sparagrass bed. It's behind the French beans which are six feet tall or more, but I could see all that went on through 'em.'

'Tell me exactly all you saw.'

More hesitation.

'I shouldn't be tellin' what goes on in private at the house. It's not right. I'd lose me job if she knew.'

It looked very much as if he was going to lose it in any case!

'You can tell me safely. I just want to know how Harry Quill spent the day before he died. We've got to know all he did. It might lead us to finding out why he died later that night and who did it.'

Lingard's inner battle seemed to resolve itself.

'Well there wasn't much. Quill went in. Mrs. Quill let him in. It was Mary's half-day off. That's the maid. They went in the drawin'-room. That's on the side of the house, overlookin' the vegetable garden where I was. There's a French window in it and I could see all that went on through it. They seemed to be talkin' quite all right. Harry kept nodding and smiling and she kept talkin' and not smilin'. When she smiles, there's usually trouble brewing. Her desk is in front of the window and she sits with her back to the garden because she says she likes the light fallin' over her shoulders. She tells me that every time she orders me to clean the windows.'

'When did they start to quarrel?'

'The telephone's in the hall. It rang. I could hear it from where I was. She went and answered it. She wasn't long, and was back mighty quick and turned on Harry. She was in one of her tantrums. I know 'em. She's like a wild thing. Harry kept listenin' and smilin' still and tryin' to get a word in edgeways. They was both standin' in the end, shoutin' at each other. She was on her feet and ravin' at him, just like she sometimes does at me when the garden's not to her satisfaction. And then Harry started ravin' too. Then she hit him across the head with her stick.'

'Did Harry make any show of violence; try to hit her, too, or get hold of her?'

'No. He just stood, with the desk between him and her, and looked to be yellin' across it at her. I didn't hear what they said. Too far away.'

'Tell me again what Harry did after the blow?'

'He sat down in a chair opposite her and put his hands to his head and then bent over the desk, sort of rubbin' where she'd hit him.'

'And then?'

'Well, I thought I'd seen enough. More than I was supposed to. If she'd seen me peeping from behind the French beans, she'd have given me the sack. So, I just made myself scarce and went and sat in the tool-shed sorting out some tulip bulbs and getting me tools clean ready for off.'

'What time would it be when they quarrelled?'

'About five. I looked at me watch as I went to the tool shed.'

'And that was all?'

'Except that Harry must have recovered from it. He must have been there on business and able to carry on. Because as I was ready for leavin', Mrs. Quill's lawyer came in through the gate. He didn't see me. I kept out of the way.'

'Mr. Nunn?'

'No. The little chap with the beard that always deals with Mrs. Quill's business.'

'Bilbow?'

'That's the one. Bilbow.'

'What time was that?'

'I told you. About six o'clock, as I was ready to leave. I'd been working a bit later.'

'And that was all?'

'I think I've said enough already. If she gets to know, it'll be the push for me. You'd better not tell her I told you all this. It must have been the ale that loosed my tongue. I'd better be going before I get myself in trouble.'

He rose a bit unsteadily, for he'd had a pint or two before he'd started on the festival brew.

'You'd better show me how to find Longton Lodge before you go.'

'That's easy. See the lane across there? First house along that. You can't miss it.'

'Why didn't you tell all this to the police before?'

'Didn't know they'd be interested. In the first place, I wasn't supposed to be watching what went on; and in the second, they said that Harry Quill didn't die till about eight o'clock that night, so it couldn't have been Mrs. Quill's hittin' him that killed him, could it? That was between five and six o'clock. Keep me out of this. I don't want mixin' up with family violence...'

He shambled off without another word.

Longton Lodge was a small Georgian place, acquired by Algy Quill through foreclosing on a mortgage. It stood back from the road, a square house with a pillared porch and about an acre of garden. The grounds must have kept Lingard busy. The flower beds in front reminded Littlejohn of a seedsman's catalogue or those little illustrated packets of seeds sold in stores for amateurs. A background like a jungle of flowering bushes and then a foreground of roses and what seemed to be every type of plant and flower, known and unknown, as though somebody had mixed up all the seeds and scattered them broadcast. The effect was not bad at all.

An elderly maid answered the bell and Littlejohn gave her his card. She returned almost at once, took his hat and led him into the drawing-room, which Lingard had already mentioned. He saw the french window and the bean-rows beyond before Mrs. Quill rose from the desk to greet him.

'I was sure you'd call, but you should have telephoned to let me know. Luckily I'm in and not occupied. Take a seat.'

She pointed to the one opposite her own at the desk, the chair in which Harry Quill had collapsed after the blow. This was evidently not going to be a comfortable fireside chat, but an interview conducted in formal fashion.

Clara Quill wore black, which suited her. She looked better without the hat and coat she'd worn at the funeral and afterwards. The tired look of when last he saw her had gone as well. Nobody quite knew her age, but it was said she was nearing eighty. She didn't look it this afternoon. She seemed fresh and business-like.

There were no handshakes. There was no warmth at all about Aunt Clara. She seemed to have no friends and the family mainly regarded her with respect and a little fear. She sat calmly in her chair, an ironical smile on her thin pale lips, her small dry hands crossed in front of her on the desk. Littlejohn might have arrived to be interviewed for a job.

'I wished to see you for a general talk about Harry's death. I wish you to understand that this affair must be treated with discretion by the police. I don't want any scandals or gossip to be bandied about concerning the Quills. This must not be the occasion for dirty linen to be washed in public.'

She looked him full in the face. Her eyes were hard and dark, with a network of small red veins across the whites and dark rings beneath them.

'We aren't in the habit of committing indiscretions of that kind, Mrs. Quill. I wish you to understand that I have not called here to be told how the police must behave. This is a murder case and we have to explore every angle of it. My visit is to ask you for certain information. I have not been called before you to receive orders.'

Her eyes lit up. She enjoyed a fight, especially with an opponent worthy of her steel.

'So! You are going to treat me as a hostile witness, are you? We'll see. What do you want?'

'We are trying to construct a schedule of Harry Quill's movements on the day he died. We can account for them until around three o'clock. From then onwards, we are not quite sure. We know he left Marcroft between two-thirty and three and we have reason to believe he came straight here to see you. Am I right?'

'Yes. Why should I deny it? Where did you obtain that information?'

There was a pack of cards on the desk. Presumably she played patience sometimes. She now drew them to her and began to finger them, running her thumb along the edge of the pack which made a purring noise which was irritating.

'It was quite easily come by. He had lunched with Rose Coggins and left her to collect some money he was expecting. As you had previously told me you were making a loan against a mortgage on his farm, I concluded that he was calling on you. When last we met, you told me Harry had taken the loan in cash already. But Rose Coggins said he was going to collect it when he left her...'

'I see. So, his kept woman has been helping you. Do you wonder that I asked you to be discreet?'

'In a case like this, we have to obtain our information from every available source. Did he call for the cash, or had you given it to him already?'

'I would rather explain that in Nunn's presence. We will leave it at that.'

She had now picked up the cards and slowly began to shuffle them.

'What time did Harry Quill leave you?'

'I don't know the exact time. The interview was a short one. It probably lasted half an hour. As you will see, the clock on the mantelpiece is broken and I don't wear a watch.'

'What happened after the interview terminated?'

'He left the room and I didn't see him again. I can't help you to complete your schedule.'

'Did he take the promised money with him? For my purposes we'll assume he hadn't received it beforehand. I understand you were to pay him in cash as he didn't have a banking account.'

'Who told you that?'

'You told me yourself. So did Miss Coggins.'

'Why ask me again then? It seems you prefer to ask that woman first about everything. Go back to your barmaid for help. I've none to give you.'

She was now looking at the cards as though she'd lost all interest in her visitor.

'Very well. Let me ask you one more question. Is it not true that Harry Quill remained in this house much longer than half an hour? He arrived around four. Why, then, was his tractor, on which he did all his travelling, still on your premises until well after six, within sight of passers-by?'

'Trespassers, you mean. It was parked in the stables out of the view of what you call passers-by. I told him to put it there as I wasn't going to have it disfiguring my front drive. I don't know how long it was there…'

'But we do. It was there until later that night, when someone called and took it back to Great Lands. Harry Quill, by then, was incapable of driving it there himself.'

She suddenly became quite still and then banged the cards down on the desk again.

'You are going too far. I must ask you to leave.'

'I'm sorry, Mrs. Quill, but I intend to remain until you give me true answers to my questions. You are evading the truth.'

'I cannot put you out myself, but I can take steps to make you regret your decision. I will answer no more questions without my lawyer.'

'I have no objection to that...'

Littlejohn looked at his watch. 4.50. He'd arranged to ring up Cromwell at Nunn's office at five. He hoped he'd gone ahead with their plans.

'In fact, I'll ring Nunn for you. May I use your telephone? I see it's in the hall.'

'I will do it myself...'

But he was half-way to the door and had the instrument in his hand when she reached him.

'Give me that telephone...'

He ignored her and gave the number of Nunn's office. Luckily it was on a card, along with others on the table which held the instrument.

'Is Inspector Cromwell with Mr. Bilbow? May I speak with him...?'

There was a pause, then Bilbow's voice. Littlejohn asked for Cromwell.

'I'm just ringing you from Mrs. Clara Quill's home at Longton Curlieu. Mrs. Quill has been giving me some information which will help us very much. I'd like you to come over here right away and we'll have it in writing. Is everything all right with you? Good. Tell Bilbow I'm here and bring him with you. Mrs. Quill says she needs his advice.'

He hung up.

During all this, Clara Quill had been standing, her weight on her heavy stick, her lips compressed.

'I won't have Bilbow. I want Nunn.'

'Mr. Nunn isn't available...'

'How do you know? You didn't ask for him.'

She was white with rage and her hands trembled on the handle of the stick. Then she took up the instrument herself.

'I wouldn't do that Mrs. Quill. Bilbow is the man you require. He's just told Inspector Cromwell all that happened between Harry Quill's arriving here and leaving again. You won't want Mr. Nunn present whilst you sort it out between you. Bilbow is on the way with my colleague. Meanwhile let's return to your desk and our business. It can't be transacted here in the hall within the hearing of servants.'

She didn't answer but reluctantly hobbled back in the drawing-room and resumed her place.

'Come here, you bungling policeman!'

She wasn't going to give up without a fight.

He followed her in, but before sitting down again, he took from her the ebony stick which she was still holding.

'Allow me to put your stick in a safe place for you, Mrs. Quill. It seems you have a habit of using it on those who displease you.'

He crossed and put it in the corner behind her.

'What do you mean? Give me back that stick. This amounts to a personal assault.'

'I've no intention that you shall assault me with it, as you did Harry Quill!'

'What is this about assaulting Harry Quill?'

'It is no use your looking angry and surprised, madam. It is true and you know it. I must now tell you that my colleague, Inspector Cromwell, has interviewed Bilbow, who has filled in most of the gaps in the schedule of Harry Quill's movements on his last day alive. Bilbow has made a full statement. He will be arrested and, Mrs. Quill, so will you. Bilbow, according to his story, was plainly an accessory to the murder of Harry Quill. *You*, however, murdered him.'

She sat there with her eyes fixed on him and full of hatred and yet she didn't seem greatly disturbed by what he was saying. He might not have been accusing her at all.

'So, Bilbow has been trying to incriminate me in his dirty work, has he?'

She paused.

'Very well. We shall see when he arrives. I don't intend to say another word about this affair until I can face him and expose him.'

'Meanwhile, Mrs. Quill, let me complete the schedule of Harry Quill's pilgrimage on the day of his death...'

'Please yourself. As I want no further conversation with you until Bilbow arrives, you may as well occupy the time proving how clever you've been.'

'Harry Quill, after leaving Rose Coggins in Marcroft, arrived here... let us say about four o'clock. He parked his tractor in the stables. He then came in the house and you talked for almost an hour. At the end of that time, the telephone rang and you answered it...'

She looked at him in surprise, baffled by his intimate knowledge of what went on. But she seemed determined not to speak.

'Meanwhile, things had been happening in Marcroft. Rose Coggins paid a hurried visit to Mr. Bilbow. Before he left her to come to Longton Lodge, Harry Quill discussed the prospects of setting Rose up in a small business. He had, it seemed, grown jealous of her contacts as a barmaid and wished to establish her in more respectable and safer work.'

A contemptuous snort from Aunt Clara, but nothing more. She was determined to maintain her ban of silence.

'Harry apparently had no idea what the nature of the business for Rose must be. Anything to get her away from the *Drovers Inn*. And he left her still undecided about it. As soon as he'd gone, Rose hurried to Bilbow for advice and told him the full tale. She trusted him and thought he could help her. Immediately after he'd got full information about Harry's plans, Bilbow telephoned to you. He told you that Harry had no intention of using the two thousand you were lending him for developing Great Lands. Instead, he was going to invest it in a modest shopkeeping business in Rose's name. In other words, he was going to give her what he borrowed from you. This information reached you when Harry was here, sitting in this very chair. You were furious and accused him of cheating you. I suppose you also began to blackguard Rose and one thing followed another until in the end you struck Harry over the head with your stick. You don't know the full details of the post-mortem, do you?'

She was dying to speak, but anxious too to show no weakness, no going back on her vow of silence. She ignored the question.

'The autopsy revealed that the blow you struck didn't kill Harry outright. I've no doubt that, at first, he behaved like anybody else who'd received a blow on the head which didn't fracture the skull. A bit confused, perhaps giddy, or even semi-conscious for a while. I wasn't there so don't know quite how it took him. But the blow had caused serious brain haemorrhage, Harry's condition gradually deteriorated, he became unconscious and finally, in a coma, he died. Those are the facts. He died here. You were alone with him as he grew worse. You didn't know what to do. So, you sent for Bilbow. I wonder what hold you have over Bilbow which made him risk his neck in the ghastly and dangerous task you prevailed on him to undertake. He had to wait until dark made the work safe and then take Harry Quill and his tractor and leave them at Great Lands, as though Harry had died on his own premises. Bilbow carried out his mission and you both hoped the police would think it was yet another crime by the prevailing black gang.

'You daren't send Harry to hospital. There would have been too many questions. If he recovered he'd certainly tell how the whole business arose; if he died in hospital, you'd have a lot of explaining to do. So you did nothing and let Harry die. I don't know whether or not he was actually dead when you put him on his own tractor and Bilbow took him for that awful last journey. It really makes no difference now. You killed Harry Quill and Bilbow was your accessory.'

There was a tap on the door, and Mary, the maid put in her head.

'Excuse me, madam. Shall I serve tea?'

Littlejohn could have laughed outright. It was well past teatime and probably the girl had been wondering why Aunt Clara hadn't rung. And now the old woman, sworn to silence until Bilbow arrived and rigidly maintaining it against all the damning details of Littlejohn's monologue, was invited to serve her tormentor with afternoon tea.

Clara Quill glared at Mary, who stood transfixed by the look, and then furiously waved her out. The front doorbell rang as the maid vanished, as though bringing down the curtain on an unpleasant second act.

Chapter XIII
Order out of Confusion

Poor Mary hardly dared enter again. She put her head round the door.

'Mr Bilbow and another gentleman.'

Bilbow's name acted like the magic word. Mrs. Quill spoke again.

'Show them in.'

She stood waiting for the newcomers, her eyes on the doorway and as soon as Bilbow entered she greeted him.

'So you decided to turn Queen's evidence, Bilbow, did you? You little rogue. What have you been telling the police about me and Harry Quill?'

Bilbow looked all in. He'd been trying to sort out the whole affair on his way to Longton Lodge and wondering how to parry the blows the police seemed to be raining on his head from all directions. Added to that, he'd been drinking most of the day and now he was in the half-world created by alcohol, where values seem all different and the edges of everything seem frayed and blurred.

He greeted Mrs. Quill's abusive welcome with a noisy response and a few shots of his own.

'Who are you calling a little rogue, you wicked old woman? And who's talking about Queen's Evidence? If you knew your law, my dear Mrs. Quill, you'd know that Queen's evidence involves an accomplice who becomes a witness against his fellows. I'm no accomplice of yours, nor am I a fellow of yours...'

'Be quiet, you drunken sot and sit down. I sent for you to...'

'You didn't send for me. I've arrived with the police. And when I return, Inspector Cromwell tells me it will be under arrest. As a lawyer, I've naturally been giving that a good deal of thought and it seems to me there's no way of avoiding it for the present. Please don't interrupt. My days of being browbeaten by you are over. You'll just listen to what I have to say and then you can tell the police anything you like. I'll make this as brief as possible...'

They faced each other like a couple of antagonistic politicians each eager to demolish what the other said.

'I shall speak to Nunn about this as soon as possible. Does he know you've called here hoping to involve me in your stupid behaviour on the night Harry Quill died?'

'He knows I'm here. I left a message and told him where I was going with the police.'

'And what lies have you been telling the police, may I ask? Superintendent Littlejohn was indulging in a long rigmarole before you arrived. Presumably you had lodged that information to save your own skin. All that nonsense about my hitting Harry with my stick and his lapsing into a coma and dying. You have a very fertile brain, Bilbow, but this time...'

'I told the police no such thing. I telephoned you that afternoon and told you that Harry was going to make a gift of your two thousand pounds loan to Rose Coggins. I thought it my duty to do so, as we were your solicitors...'

'Nunn is my lawyer. You are merely his lackey, running errands.'

She was working herself into a fury again and froth gathered at the corners of her lips. She wiped it off with a sweep of her handkerchief.

'Lackey or not, I'm not running any more of your errands. And let me speak, and stop interrupting. I'm determined to tell my share of that night's events in the presence of the police, whatever it costs me. First of all, let me tell them how you prevailed on me to do your dirty work...'

In the fury of his dilemma, he seemed to have recovered his wits. The effects of his whisky were wearing off and he didn't seem to make any effort to brace himself by further drinking. Cromwell could see the outline of his flask in his hip pocket, but Bilbow showed no inclination to use it.

'As far as I am concerned my tattered position and reputation in the law is finally destroyed. I cannot harm myself further by telling the police why I have tolerated your bullying and insults for so long.'

Mrs. Quill, for the first time, manifested signs of distress. Her bold front was showing fissures at last.

'Stop,' she said. 'You had better keep quiet. You know what this will mean?'

Bilbow remained quite calm. He even showed a little unexpected dignity.

'In your strong box at the bank, you hold a cheque for a thousand pounds, payable to me, drawn on your own account and handed to you by your bank after payment. Attached to that cheque is a letter from me, referring to the cheque and stating that it was for an interest-free loan from you to me to enable me to pay off a discrepancy in the books of Nunn and Company, for which I was responsible. When I appealed to you for help five years ago, it was either prison or your mercy. God! I wish I'd chosen prison. You established a hold over me then which has totally ruined me.

Thanks to Mr. Nunn, I had been able to recover somewhat from the wreck of my past. You simply thrust me back in the mud from which I'd crawled. Now be quiet. The police are going to hear what I have to say, either here or at the police station, where I hope I shall still have your company after they've arrested you. Last Tuesday, late in the afternoon, you telephoned me to insist that I called on you right away. I knew it was for something disreputable, as usual. When I arrived, I found you with Harry Quill in this room. He was lying on the floor unconscious. You hadn't even had the decency to lay him on the couch or even put a cushion under his head. You said that after my message by telephone, you had faced Harry with the fact that he was going to use your loan for Rosie and not for the improvement of his farm. He had grown furious in an argument which followed and threatened you with violence. In the heat of the quarrel, you had defended yourself with your stick and he had fallen and struck his head on the desk.'

'That is all lies and exaggeration ... I ...'

Bilbow shouted her down.

'It was not. And let me speak.'

Littlejohn and Cromwell merely stood as spectators, listening to the duel going on between the two angry antagonists. The police might not have been there at all. Bilbow and Mrs. Quill had forgotten them in the heat of combat which would destroy either or both of them.

'I suggested we sent for the doctor. But you would have none of it. You weren't, you said, going to have the whole affair aired in court, where it would surely end if outside help were called for. You used your usual threat. Either I did as you wished, or ... I was foolish enough to agree finally to what you wanted.'

He turned to Littlejohn.

'This, Chief Superintendent, is the truth, to which I will swear in court, if necessary. Clara Quill's plan was that we wait until after dark and then I should take Harry Quill on his own tractor and place him on his own doorstep and leave him there, thus disposing of him and his vehicle. I said I would do no such thing, whatever the consequences. She then agreed that I could do what I wished with him, provided I took him and his vehicle off her premises and freed her from any connection with Harry or his condition. I finally agreed. My full intention was that on leaving and getting away from her abominable influence, I would take him to Marcroft, call the ambulance and say I had found him in the road beside his tractor, which I proposed to overturn, and make it appear he had fallen and injured himself in the accident. I could see that Harry was in poor shape and I was anxious to get away, but my plan involved being in the dark where I could act without being seen concocting the mishap. As we waited, Harry Quill died.'

His presentation of the facts and his fluent description of the appalling situation in which they had found themselves seemed to stun even Clara Quill. She stood staring at Bilbow without even trying to deny it.

Bilbow shrugged his shoulders.

'In those circumstances, Clara Quill's original plan seemed the best way out for both of us. She pressed me to fall in with it. After all, she said, there was an epidemic of farm robberies with violence. Why shouldn't Harry Quill have fallen a victim of the Black Gang?'

He turned to Littlejohn and Cromwell again.

'That's all. You know the rest. I was in such a state after I left this infernal house that I couldn't see the thing through without a drink whatever the risk. At the *Dick Turpin* I encountered bad luck. I fumbled my way out of the car park on Harry's tractor, with his body tied to it wrapped in old sacks. She wouldn't even provide him with decent covering in case it incriminated her.'

He finished abruptly and stood there, his head hanging, like a guilty prisoner in the dock.

'I'm sorry that, to save my own skin, I committed an unpardonable crime. Harry Quill had been a friend of mine...'

There was a decanter of brandy on a silver tray on a side table. Cromwell half-filled a glass with it and handed it to Bilbow, who gave him a thin smile of acknowledgement and then drank it slowly.

Littlejohn turned to Clara Quill who was now sitting at her desk shuffling her playing cards, pretending to be calm.

'Have you anything to say?'

'Harry Quill was a disgrace. Bilbow is a bigger one. The whole of his rigmarole is a pack of lies. I am not going to make a forensic *tour de force*, as he has done to try to persuade you of my innocence. I will just say this. Harry Quill called here for his money, which I had, as promised, drawn from the bank in cash. We talked and I gave him what I thought good advice about what to do with it. He said he'd remember what I said and was unusually polite, good humoured, smiling, as well he might be in the circumstances. As I was about to give him the money from my safe, the telephone bell rang. It was Bilbow advising me not to pay Harry, as he'd received information that he proposed to spend the money on Rose Coggins. I thereupon faced Harry with the news, he argued and finally admitted it was true. He also told a pitiable tale about his life at Great Lands with Millie and began to praise Rose to the skies. I cut him short, gave him my own opinion of her and we quarrelled furiously. Finally, he started to make insinuations about the life my late husband and I led before we married and compared it with his own present arrangements. I was so incensed that I struck him across the face with my stick. Then occurred what usually does after violence in a quarrel. The whole of it died down, he took it well, he wasn't hurt and he sat in that chair by the fireplace to recover. He drank two glasses of brandy and soda and seemed to like it. He took two more and then talked of leaving. By then, being unused to strong drink, he was half drunk. I considered it dangerous for him to attempt to drive that ramshackle tractor home. I telephoned for Bilbow to come and attend to it. He arrived. They left at about seven o'clock. Harry sitting on a pile of sacks on the back, Bilbow driving. That was the last I saw of Harry alive.'

Littlejohn turned to her. 'What about the money?'

'I felt sorry for Harry, somehow. But, in a gush of pity, I'd no intention of handing him two thousand pounds to throw away on that woman. He had already signed the mortgage deed, however, and I said I'd think it over and see him again in two days. All that, in front of Bilbow, who, I don't suppose will confirm it in the present circumstances.'

'I won't confirm it because it's a fabrication...'

'Wait!' said Littlejohn. 'There's something I've forgotten. I've an errand to make and I'll be back here in half an hour. Meanwhile, you, Bilbow and Mrs. Quill will wait with Inspector Cromwell and unless I have your word to remain quietly as you are, I shall send for the village constable to stand in with him. Well?'

'We have no choice.'

The pair of them agreed for once.

Littlejohn covered the distance to Marcroft in twelve minutes in the police car and drew up at the *Drovers* just after opening time.

Mr. Criggan was very annoyed about his visit.

'We've only just opened and Rosie's only just got here.'

'Send her to me without delay.'

Mr. Criggan obeyed with a surly gesture.

'Come in here, Rose...'

She looked alarmed, especially when Littlejohn closed the door.

'What...?'

'Look here, my girl, suppose you tell me the truth for once. When you visited Bilbow on the afternoon before Harry Quill died, you didn't go for advice about what sort of a business to buy, did you? You went to inform your lover what Harry proposed to do. Give you money and get you out of town in a shop of some kind... Now don't tell me any more lies. Bilbow is in danger of being arrested for murdering Harry Quill...'

She turned white and her mouth opened wide.

'He never...'

'Tell me now, he was your lover, wasn't he?'

She began to weep, tears rolling uncontrolled down her cheeks. She brushed them away with her hand.

'You seem to know all about it. We are lovers. Have been for a long time. We'd have been married if his wife had divorced him, but she wouldn't.'

'What about Harry Quill?'

'Him! I never loved him. We were just friends and he used to give me things and help me along when I needed it...'

'He was going to give you the money he so badly needed for his farm?'

'That was his business.'

'What did Bilbow say about all this?'

'He was mad about me, too. But I loved him. It wasn't like Harry. I was just sorry for Harry. Bilbow was terribly jealous of other men. That's why I gave up Tim. Harry was different. He was just a joke.'

'You kept it very quiet, you and Bilbow.'

'We had to. It wouldn't have done for him to be talked about in the town.'

'Why?'

'He'd have lost his job. He was a prominent solicitor. You know that. He'd have had hard work finding another.'

'I'm sure he would. And he'd have had no money, would he?'

She had stopped her weeping and now her face was hard.

'No need to insult me. I've had my bad times like anybody else. I've no intention of not knowing where my next meal was coming from like I did after Jack died. He used to say how much he loved me and he left me penniless. I've learned to know what men mean when they say they love you. What about Bilbow?'

'I've no time to discuss that now. You'd better get back to the bar, Rose. Mr. Criggan will be annoyed with us.'

He left her and was back at Longton Lodge a quarter of an hour later.

Cromwell had called in the village constable after all. He was sitting stiffly there, his helmet on his knees, looking with silent apprehension at Mrs. Quill, who was feared very much in the locality.

Cromwell thanked and dismissed him before explaining his presence there.

'Mr. Bilbow threatened to leave the house if you weren't back in a quarter of an hour. I thought I'd better call in the local police and have him detained.'

Bilbow seemed too angry to take any notice of Cromwell. He hurried across the room to Littlejohn.

'What's the meaning of all this? Leaving us in the air and going off like that. I don't know what Mrs. Quill thinks about it, but I think it's a damn' bad show.'

Mrs. Quill didn't say anything. She had passed the time by playing a game of patience and was wondering whether to cheat herself or not and get it over.

'I've been to Marcroft. To the *Drovers Inn,* in fact. I wanted to make a few more enquiries from Rose Coggins.'

Mrs. Quill looked up impatiently from her game.

'That woman again. I can't see what you men can see in her.'

Bilbow shouted above her voice.

'What have you been pestering her again for? Hasn't she had enough trouble without the police hounding her out of her wits? What have you been up to?'

'I'll tell you, Bilbow. I listened patiently to the verbal duel between you and Mrs. Quill. Each of you blamed the other and your testimonies didn't tally at all. Some of what you said bore out our own discoveries. For example, Mrs. Quill said she gave Harry plenty of brandy to revive him. Had he been unconscious, he couldn't have taken enough to make him drunk.'

'How do you know he took it at all or that she gave it to him? And how do you know he was drunk?'

'The autopsy showed that he hadn't eaten since his meal at lunch time. His aunt hadn't been hospitable, and his stomach was empty. Except that there was a considerable quantity of brandy there. Enough to make one unaccustomed to alcohol, half-drunk at least.'

'So you went to ask Rose if he'd had brandy at her place. That was clever of you, I must say. Just a waste of time.'

'I didn't go for that at all. Your emotional and insincere forensic effort before I left, when you spoke like a lawyer playing on the feelings of a jury...'

'As Mr. Bilbow told me,' Cromwell added, 'like Marshall Hall. He thought such methods old-fashioned.'

'I wished to be sure about another type of emotion connected with you, Bilbow. Your relations with Rose Coggins. It suddenly struck me that Rose was very eager to run to you for advice after Harry had told her about buying a business for her. He hadn't even got the money then. She admitted, when I asked her, that you were her lover. She felt she was getting in too deeply with Harry and wanted you to know...

'It's a pack of lies. You have no right to bully witnesses, which I'm sure you did. I shall see to this...'

'Do that, Mr. Bilbow. But now we know why you rang up Mrs. Quill and told her what Harry was going to do with her loan. You wanted to prevent his getting the money.'

'I wished to warn Mrs. Quill that her cash would be put to an improper purpose.'

'That was very considerate of you, Bilbow...'

Mrs. Quill looked at him over the tops of the glasses she had put on.

'... Especially after the way I'd blackmailed you about the cheque and the letter you signed. You fool! I destroyed both years ago. After Nunn had informed me you had put right the books. When your defalcations were discovered, Nunn told me. It was I who persuaded him to keep you on his staff even then. Nunn was going to have you gaoled. Perhaps it slipped your attention that about that time a cashier was taken on who relieved you of all contacts with money of any kind and your skill was confined to the law alone.'

'You didn't tell me...'

'Of course I didn't. I wanted to be sure you'd behave yourself in future. You were saying, Superintendent...?'

'I was going to remark that, having stopped Harry Quill from receiving the money, Bilbow didn't seem to have a motive for killing him. Then I thought about Rose Coggins. Perhaps Bilbow and Quill were rivals. Had Quill gone too far in offering Rose all that money? Apparently he had in Bilbow's opinion. He killed him for it...'

'You can't prove that. It's as I said, Clara Quill did it and I got her out of the mess she'd made.'

Littlejohn went on as though Bilbow hadn't interrupted.

'And all to no purpose. She and Harry were just friends, Rose told me, and she never loved him. He gave her things and helped her along. He was going to give her all he had; and she told me Harry was just a joke. It may have been all lies. She's a natural liar. She'll even send Bilbow to gaol for life if it suits her.'

'She loves me. We'd be married...'

'Rubbish. She's just anybody's woman. Anybody with money to give her. She'd actually have taken all Harry had and then thrown him aside, just as she will do to you, Bilbow, when you go to gaol.'

Cromwell had seized the little lawyer's arm when he showed signs of rushing at Littlejohn, and held him fast. Bilbow was frothing at the mouth.

'Lies! You're making it all up to incriminate me...'

'Let me quote her again, when I asked her about her feelings about you. She said "I've no intention of not knowing where my next meal's coming from... I've learned to know what men are when they say they love you." Ask her if she comes to see you in prison, which I'm afraid she won't. Or better still, I'll arrange for you to see her tonight. Will that do?'

'I don't believe it!'

'You, Bilbow, Tim Quill, Harry Quill and who else besides? She said Harry was a joke. She'll tell the next man you all were a joke. And he'll believe her, like you did, Bilbow.'

Bilbow made for the nearest chair and sat down heavily. He looked at Mrs. Quill, engaged in a new game of patience as though no cloud hung over her at all.

'So you destroyed the letter and the cheque. Is that true?'

'I'm not a liar, Bilbow. You can ask Nunn. He'll tell you of the pressure I successfully exerted to get you another chance. That woman seems to have ruined it all.'

'Leave that out of it. Why did you do it?'

'Nunn liked you and admired your brains. I liked you, and strange to say, I admired your lack of bitterness and your fortitude in the face of the raw deal life gave you. I found out all about you. Your wife was no good. She ran away with your partner, but you didn't divorce her because you thought she'd come back. You knew your partner's predatory nature. You took the blame. She died, didn't she, instead, and you turned to whisky and finally to a trollop like Rose for consolation. I didn't know about Rose. That was the last straw.'

Bilbow, who had hitherto resisted the brandy bottle, seized it.

'Do you mind?'

'Take some if it will help you.'

He took a good half tumblerful. He paused and then spoke quietly.

'And now, I'll tell you what really happened. After all the noise and confused accounts you'll probably not believe me. She... Mrs. Quill had nothing to do with it. Harry Quill was quite conscious and well when I arrived. He'd recovered from the blow Mrs. Quill gave him, but he was drunk. I did drive the tractor with Harry Quill as a passenger. He was quite incapable of doing it himself. A drunken teetotaller! I'd got to take him by the roads where I wouldn't meet the police. I was drunk in my car last New Year's Eve and my licence was suspended for a year. On the way, Harry began to talk. He seemed quite cheerful. I expect it was the brandy. He thanked me for helping him with Mrs. Quill. Yes, he did. And he said he was sure that next time they met he'd be able to persuade her to grant him the loan. "I'll offer to give up Rose and get on with the farming and when I've set Rose up in her business, somewhere far enough away from here, I'll be able to go and see her just the same." And he came out with a lot of silly drunken talk about Rose and about their relationship. I couldn't stand it any more. I stopped the tractor and hit him. He was still unsteady and fell backwards and hit his head against the steel chassis. He just lay there, unconscious.'

Bilbow took another good drink and nobody tried to prevent him.

'I didn't know what to do. It was still daylight. I tried to bring him round, but couldn't.'

'Where was that?'

'Near the *Jolly Tinker* crossroads, on the back road to Marcroft. There were a few cars about, so I took Harry and the tractor through a gateway and hid them behind the hedge of a field until it was dark enough to move on again. I did all I could for him, in the circumstances. I was in a real mess. I ought to have taken him to Marcroft Hospital, but I couldn't muster the courage. Instead, I went in the inn there and got a drink. When I returned a few minutes later, Harry had died. You know the rest. All that stupid and nightmare journey to Great Lands...'

He looked across at Mrs. Quill who was no longer playing cards, and nodded at her.

'One good turn deserves another. You had nothing to do with Harry's death. You know how to put the fear of God in people, waving that stick, but you haven't the strength to swat a fly with it. You'd marked his head a bit with the blow, but the rubber ferrule prevented it being a bad one. He was quite fit and well until I hit him and he caught his head on the tractor...'

Bilbow got away with manslaughter and a five year sentence. Nunn and Clara Quill visit him in prison and will probably see him right in some way when he's free again. Rose Coggins married a bookmaker not long after the trial. He gives her the things that help her along and, now and then, gives her a good hiding to show who's master.

Following Bilbow's arrest, Mr. Nunn had a quiet talk with Littlejohn.

'Mrs. Quill has asked me to apologise to you for the wrong information she gave you when you first met at the hotel. You will doubtless recollect that she told you that Harry Quill had already received the cash for the £2,000 loan she had arranged to make him, when all the time, he hadn't yet had it...'

'I do remember, Mr. Nunn, and, although I guessed the reason for the lies she told me... I can describe them as nothing else... I was going to call on her for an explanation.'

'She has asked me to tender it, and apologise sincerely on her behalf. She is an old woman and had taken too much brandy when you interviewed her. She asks if you will overlook it.'

'Of course. I'll forget it in the circumstances.'

Nunn gave him a slow smile.

'Between you and me, Littlejohn, and now that it's all over, she's a fine business woman. Harry Quill, at the time of his death, hadn't taken his loan. The mortgage, although already signed and in my hands, was void, and Clara wouldn't get Great Lands as she'd planned. It was a good investment at the price she was paying and she greatly coveted it. She thought that if she said she'd paid the money over to Harry before his death, she'd still get Great Lands and that I would help her to do it. Nobody but herself, Bilbow and I knew he hadn't had the loan. There are limits to what I will do for Mrs. Quill. My apologies, too, for not interfering with her statement at the time she made it to you. I did interfere later...'

Harry Quill's will was never found, so Rose Coggins derived no benefit from his death. But a piece of strange irony finally rang down the curtain on the case.

When it came time to remove the remains of the burned-out haystack, used by Mrs. Quill to give the alarm of Harry's death, the workmen who did it came upon a small locked deed-box, externally undamaged except that the enamel had all peeled off among the ashes. They handed it to Mr. Nunn. When it was forced open, it revealed that Harry Quill must still have had some money tucked away in a hiding place nobody had thought of, the heart of a haystack. When the scorched contents, which consisted of a pile of thoroughly toasted, ghostly looking banknotes, encountered the open air, they crumbled away to dust. There was what appeared to be one other document with them. To Mr. Nunn, it looked very much like Harry Quill's will, but, to his relief, it also disintegrated into grey unrecognisable powder before it could be identified.

The Night They Killed Joss Varran

George Bellairs

CHAPTER I
THE WAITING WOMAN

Crouched in a dead hamlet in the harshest part of the Ballaugh marshes, locally known as the Curraghs, Close Dhoo cottage was a sad little place which none of the changing seasons seemed to cheer. Always the same in all weathers, with its desolate front garden, its barren trees and its tightly closed door, with the paint peeling off it. The small windows with their shabby curtains hid all that went on inside. The roof, once thatched, was now covered in tarred corrugated iron through which the rust of decay was beginning to show.

The place, once a croft, occupied a small patch of poor ground of under an acre parallel with a shabby, unmetalled road leading farther into the marshes, with a barren garden behind littered with rubbish – ashes, tin cans, old iron and shards of pottery, and a long alley down the middle receding into the wilderness. Its boundaries were marked by old struggling hawthorn bushes leaning at an angle from the prevailing wind. The garden was completely neglected but, in Spring, the daffodils, planted by occupants long gone, bloomed in profusion and the fuchsias, as old as the house itself, blossomed unseen.

The locality was hushed and seemed to be listening for something. Once, the inhabitants of the now deserted hamlet had, as evening fell, been able to set their clocks by the whistle of the last train to Ramsey leaving the station two miles away. Now they had all gone, railway and people, except the solitary occupant of the lonely house. She was sitting in a plain wooden armchair beside the dying fire of wood in the primitive hearth, waiting. A small, prematurely aged woman, with a resigned weatherworn face in a frame of straight, grey close-cut hair. The fading light of the late autumn day dimly lit up her face and revealed the tight skin showing the bones of the skull beneath, the small thin mouth and the broad snub nose.

The interior of the house consisted of one large room, with a smaller one leading off it and a lean-to kitchen. In the background, a plank ladder led to a trap-door in the loft. The place with its simple old furniture had a dreary look. Full of memories of a departed family. Isabel Varran, the occupant, was one of a family of ten, all scattered except herself and the brother, Josiah, for whom she was now waiting. The walls of the room were decorated with old fly-blown photographs of children, wedding groups posed among absurd Victorian cardboard scenery, or of individual men and women staring with almost frightened looks at the camera behind which the photographer had counted out the interminable seconds to secure the likeness.

A ramshackle green van drew up at the gate and a hefty fat woman in an old coat and with her hair covered by a soiled gaudy scarf, emerged, wobbled up the path and entered the room without knocking at the door. The wind, the muffled drumming of which was rising, entered with her and blew the low fire into flame and drew puffs of aromatic smoke from the smouldering gorse wood into the room.

The newcomer was too inquisitive even to greet the waiting woman.

'Has Joss come yet?'

She wore old trousers and gumboots and was panting heavily from her efforts. She placed her hands flat on the table and rested her great lumbering body on her powerful arms.

The other slowly raised her head and gave her sister a weary, baffled look.

'No. I don't know what...'

The other cut her off quickly.

'Of course, you know as well as I do. The boat arrived in Douglas from Liverpool hours since. He's stopping at all the pubs on his way here. It's just like him. You'd think after more than twelve months in gaol for drunken violence, he'd have had enough. But our Joss was always too clever to learn...'

She paused to gulp in air.

'I suppose he'll be here after the pubs close. Well, I haven't time to wait. I'm going now. Sydney's been out all day. He says there's a farmers' meeting of some sort in Ramsey, but I don't know what he's up to. I've had all the milking to do. The doctor told me to take things easy. I expect that one day I'll drop down dead and that'll be the end of it.'

And with that depressing prognosis, she left as she had come, without a word of farewell. The rattle of the old van died away in the distance and silence descended again, punctuated by the steady tick-tack of the cheap alarm clock on the dresser.

Left alone, the woman remained in her chair, lost in her own thoughts, her hands together in her lap as if in prayer, except that she monotonously rotated her thumbs round one another, a habit which had been her mother's, too, when she was anxious about anything. As the last of the sad daylight faded from the room, she rose and switched on the solitary electric light which hung over the table, a single lamp in a cheap pink shade. The lamp illuminated the room more starkly than the struggling daylight and revealed the well-polished Welsh dresser, the oak corner cupboard and the worn rush-bottomed chairs.

She went again to the door, looked out and then shone a torch into the darkness. A damp smell of trees and earth from the garden entered the room. She closed the door again with an anxious forlorn gesture and went to the kitchen and filled an electric kettle and made some tea. Then she cut thick slices of bread and butter, produced some cold cooked sausages from the pantry and set out her meal on one corner of the table under the light in the living-room. She ate her meal, slowly masticating it and washing it down with draughts of tea from a large mug. She seemed lost in thought and took no interest in what she was doing. Only once did she show any sign of where her thoughts were wandering. Half-way through her feeding, she rose, paused and then went to the sideboard and took out a purse, from which she counted twenty one pound notes. She replaced three of these and with the rest in one hand, groped up the chimney of the wide hearth and with the other brought down an old metal teapot. She stuffed the money in it and replaced it. Just in case her brother indulged in his old habit of helping himself to her savings. Then she finished her tea. Twice more in the course of tidying and washing-up she went to the door and looked out into the night. There was nobody about. In the distance a dog barked and far away the headlamps of a passing car shone across the marshes, from which a thin mist was rising, and faded away. She put on a pair of spectacles and sat again in the chair by the fire, which she revived with wood from a box on the hearth, and began to read a book she had borrowed from the country library. Soon she had fallen asleep.

She moved and the book falling from her lap awakened her. She sat up with a start and looked at the clock. Five minutes past ten. She rose in a flurry and hurried to the door, gathering up the torch on her way. Outside it was pitch dark. The wind had dropped and now hissed quietly in the bushes along the road. The woman stood at the door, the light from her torch illuminating the path and the ramshackle wooden gate. She remained there for a minute, lost in thought, wondering when her brother would finally turn up. Then, almost mechanically, she moved into the dark and walked to the gate, struggled briefly with the broken catch and stepped out into the road. She shone her torch here and there and suddenly brought the beam to rest on a huddled bundle under the hedge opposite the house. She hurried across and stooped over it.

For one incredulous minute she examined what she had found and then uttered a shrill wail. It was the body of a man.

The corpse lay face downwards with arms spread above its head. All around the earth was disturbed, as though there had been a struggle or the murderer had tried to drag him further into the bushes. There was no doubt about the cause of death. There was a gaping wound in the back of the head and a streak of congealed blood running from the skull and round one side of the neck.

The woman stood for a moment panting and whimpering. The flashlight, which was almost played-out and now gave forth a faint red glimmer, fell from her hands. She did not trouble to rescue it, but first ran along the path to the house, illuminated by the light shining through the doorway, and then back to the road and vanished in the darkness.

Even in the dark, the woman knew her way about. As soon as she stepped off the rambling highway of two barely discernible tracks almost obliterated by grass and weeds, a labyrinth of corkscrew paths overhung by marsh shrubs and trees spread in every direction. Without hesitating, she made her way through the wilderness, running and then reducing her speed to a walk as she recovered her breath. Finally, she emerged on a narrow macadamed road. Almost at the junction stood a whitewashed farmstead in a large yard. Before she reached it a dog emerged boiling from his kennel, came to the end of his tether, and hurled himself savagely on his hind legs struggling to get free. As the woman entered the farmyard, a window in the house opened and a man's voice cursed the dog and yelled at him to be quiet.

Above the noise of the man and dog, the woman tried to make herself heard.

'Joss is dead. Somebody's killed him.'

The man at the window leaned out farther, peering into the dark. Suddenly wakened from his first sleep, he was bemused and he half wondered if in the confusion of its furious barking, the dog had started to articulate as well. He shouted back into the blackness.

'What do you say?'

The woman screamed this time at the top of her voice.

'Joss has been killed!'

Without another word the head above vanished and the window was slammed. A light went on in the room and was followed by one after another from other windows as the occupants awoke there. Finally, the general turmoil inside seemed to rouse the occupant of a tower erected at one end of the house and the light went on there, too, and joined the rest of the illuminations.

The woman stood motionless and dazed. Now and then she whimpered in protest at the time the occupants were taking to appear.

Suddenly the door opened and a shaft of light shot across the neat path to the large white gate and the forlorn figure of the woman waiting like a ghost near the house.

Silhouetted in the doorway stood a fat, stocky, middle-aged man in pyjama top and trousers with his braces dangling behind him like a tail. He had close-cropped hair, a stubble of iron-grey beard, large ears and a strong short neck. He rubbed the sleep from his eyes.

'Who is it?'

'Isabel Varran from Close Dhoo. Joss has been killed.'

The man grunted.

The family at Close-e-Cass scarcely knew their nearest neighbours. The Varrans were reputed to be a queer lot and Isabel was regarded as being the oddest of them.

'What did you say about Joss?'

'He's dead. Somebody killed him.'

'Where is he?'

'In the hedge opposite our house.'

'Are you sure he's dead?'

Meanwhile other members of the family had gathered round the fat man. Three men, one of whom might have been his brother and the others his sons. Joseph Candell, the fat man, didn't seem at all pleased by the disturbance and his involvement in it. He was a man of little initiative and hesitated about his next move. Meanwhile, the dog began to bark again. It gave him a chance to vent his feelings and he ran to the kennel and kicked the dog, which ran yelping for shelter.

A bell, dangling from a spring on the wall of the hall began to jangle. It was from the occupant of the strange tower, who rarely left it, and called for attention by the home-made alarm.

An elderly woman appeared, her grey hair in rollers, with a coat over her nightdress.

'What's going on here? Grandfather's getting up.'

'Go and tell him to keep out of this and be quiet.'

The woman, Candell's wife, didn't seem to hear but passed him and went to the solitary figure waiting in the dark for the next move.

'What is it, Isabel?'

At the sound of the gentle voice of the older woman, the younger one suddenly burst into noisy weeping.

'Joss is dead...'

'Come indoors out of the cold.'

She laid her hand on Isabel's shoulder and led her inside. As she passed the group of men she turned on them.

'Well, what are you lot waiting for? Get along with you to Close Dhoo and see what's been happening there. I'll make some tea for her. She can wait here.'

A figure then appeared on the landing of the wide staircase. A fierce-looking old man with a flurry of shaggy white hair, tall and stooping, dressed in a calf-length white nightshirt. It was old Junius Candell, aged about ninety, who years ago had surrendered the running of the farm and a small share of the capital and profits to his eldest son and retired to a tower which he had built on the end of the house. He spent most of his time there watching all that went on in all the fields and buildings.

'What's the hullaballo about? Nobody tells me anything.'

Old Junius waved his stick in the air. It had, in days past, been laid so often across his son's back, that the fat man at the door made an instinctive gesture with his left arm as though to ward off a blow.

The last arrival on the stairs was the fat man's daughter. She was dressed in a negligée, bought from a mail order firm and certified 'as worn by famous actresses'.

Mrs. Candell appeared to be the only person with any initiative. She turned on the two younger men.

'Get back to your room and get dressed. Somebody will have to go down to Close Dhoo and see what this is about.'

Then she addressed the girl, who was leaning against the wall half-way up the stairs, breathing on her finger nails and rubbing them on the sleeve of her *peignoir*, as the advertisement had called it.

'And you, Beulah, have you nothing better to do? See your grandfather back to his room. He'll be getting his death of cold. Tell him to get in bed.'

The old man gave the girl a toothless grin as she approached him. She was obviously the apple of his eye.

'Come on, granda. She says you're to get back to bed.'

'Eh?'

He was a bit deaf. She led him away.

The clock in the hall struck midnight. The men, who had scattered when Mrs. Candell told them to go and dress now gathered again at the door. The two sons, tall, heavy, slow moving, looked to their father for his orders. The fat man seemed to realise at last that they had better do something quickly, put on his cap and took a large stick from a collection of many generations in an umbrella stand near the front door.

'We'd better three of us go. Uncle Tom, stay with the women. We don't know who's prowling about. If what the Varran girl says is true, we ought to get the police...'

The younger of the sons, in his early twenties, with a beatnik haircut and sideboards, giggled nervously.

'We ought to be sure she's tellin' the truth, oughtn't we? If Bella Varran has imagined it all, we'll look daft when the police get here and find it's nothing but a hoax...'

'You shut up! If we leave a dead man lying in the ditch all night, we'll be in proper trouble.'

The older son, a smiling, naïve, good-tempered giant, thought he ought to say a word.

'Had I better take me gun?'

The fat man was out of patience with the whole business and wanted to get back to bed.

'What the hell would we want with a gun? Whoever's done this, if it has been done, will be miles off by now. Let's get goin'. Bring the big flashlamp...'

The fat man walked very fast and with the assurance of one who knew every step of the way. The air was still and cold and the quick clatter of the men's hobnailed boots against the loose flints of the track made them sound like a group of horses. At first, nobody spoke. The fat man breathed asthmatically through his mouth. He was still half-drunk with sleep and grumbling to himself about the ruin of his night's rest. The youngest son was talking quietly, pursuing his original train of thought.

'A lot of fine fools we'll look if...'

'Shut up and save your breath!'

Nobody knew what Joseph Candell was thinking about. Nobody ever did. He was a lumbering, slow thinking man who spoke little, had difficulty in expressing himself and grew irritable when he could not do so. Now, the pace was too fast for him. He began to wonder why he was hurrying and slackened his steps. His sons followed suit and the younger one paused to light a cigarette. They had reached the long twisting path which led to Close Dhoo and left behind the tunnel of trees which had once been planted as a part of the scheme when the great trench was dug to drain the marshes. As they reached the wider track, above which the stars were now visible, the sky seemed to pale in the direction of Ballaugh, giving an illusion that dawn was near.

A light shone out from a solitary cottage ahead of them.

'There's Close Dhoo. She must have left the light on.'

Nobody answered, but they all thought alike. Descended from a race of peasants, all waste was abhorrent to them. The three men reduced their pace, as though reluctant to face what was awaiting them. They felt like intruders in a matter which did not concern them.

The younger son, his hands in his pockets, had been whistling nervously between his teeth.

'What do we do when we get there?'

The fat man, faced with a decision, grew irritable, as usual.

'What the hell do you think we'll do? She said his body was in the ditch opposite the house. You and Baz can go and look for it. I'll go and see what's going on in the house.'

They reached the house and paused irresolutely. In the silence they could hear water babbling somewhere.

'Well? What are you two waiting for? Get on with it.'

The two Candell boys obeyed. Their nailed boots clattered across the flints and then fell silent as they met the soft mould of the hedge. Their father strode boldly up the path of trodden earth to the front door. Before entering he peeped through the window at the side, but the curtains obscured all that was within. He hesitated before trying the door and looked back to where his sons had left him. He could not see them, but the noise of crackling twigs and the dancing light of the torch they were carrying indicated that they were vigorously tackling the job in hand.

'Hey!'

The shrill shout breaking the silence pulled them up. Their father hurried down the path and found them knee-deep in the ditch.

'There's no body here. I said she'd imagined it and we'd be made to look fools...'

'Shut up! And what do you think you're doing there? If you find the dead man and the police are brought in, there'll be a hell of a row because you've trampled all over the place and spoiled the clues with your big feet...'

'Fine fools we look...'

'Shut up, I said. We ought never to have started searching for the body. And it's me who is the fool turning the pair of you loose on the job. I might have known you'd mess it up.'

He paused and blew through his mouth.

'There's only one thing for it. We'd better get the police. We can't run the risk of interfering any more. It's their responsibility. Put that light out and come back to the road...'

The three of them scrambled out of the mud and peat of the ditch and stood in the road hesitantly.

'It's as near to the village as going back home to telephone. Baz, you'd better walk down and get the policeman. I've had enough of this. Somebody else had better take the responsibility. As it is, there'll be trouble when they find how the pair of you have trampled all over the place.'

'It's a good half hour's walk from here...'

'Don't argue with me. I'd send Joe, only he won't be able to tell a proper tale. As it is, I'm sure you'll make a mess of it, too. Just go and knock up Kincaid and tell him that Isabel Varran has come and told us that she's found her brother Joss dead in the road, and he'd better come right away. Got that? Nothing else. Don't start spinning a long yarn. I know what you're like when you get talking. So watch your tongue if you don't want trouble. Bring Kincaid here. We'll wait in the house.'

Baz was too bewildered even to argue and went off in the darkness. His hobnails rang on the road and gradually receded until there was silence again.

'We'd better go in and wait. No sense in standing out here in the dark.'

They crossed the road and down the path to the house. Candell was first and fumbled with the latch.

'What the...?'

He pushed open the door and in the shaft of light from the room looked at his podgy hand.

It was covered in dark congealed blood.

He hurried indoors and his son shambled after him.

The room was as neat and tidy as Isabel Varran had left it. The table was covered with a red velvet cloth and in the middle stood a half-empty bottle of whisky without a cork.

The centre of the stage, however, was occupied by a solitary figure slumped in an arm-chair before the dead fire. The head lay on one side in an attitude of great weariness and the arms dangled one each over the arms of the chair, the hands outstretched and the soiled broken fingernails almost touching the floor.

The features were those of a man of middle age, lined and grubby, and with several days' growth of beard. The square head, with its thatch of close-cropped iron-grey hair, was thrown back and the eyes were open and staring. He wore an old suit and soiled shirt without tie. The shirt front was soaked in whisky, the reek of which filled the room, as though someone had tried to revive him by forcing it between his teeth.

The younger man stared wild-eyed at the body, his lips moving soundlessly. Then he ran out into the garden and his father could hear him retching.

The older man approached the corpse, his fat arms ahead of him, like someone forcing his way through a thick hedge. He touched the cold forehead with the flat of his hand, uttered a noise like a sob and then, with a quick gesture, closed the staring eyes with his forefinger and thumb. Then he ran to join his son outside.

Half an hour later when Baz and the village constable arrived in the latter's official car, they found the fat man and Joe sitting on the doorstep with the door locked behind them, staring into space.

Love George Bellairs? Join the Readers' Club

Get your next George Bellairs Mystery for FREE

If you sign up today, this is what you'll get:

1. A free classic Bellairs mystery, *Corpses in Enderby*;
2. Details of Bellairs' new publications and the opportunity to get copies in advance of publication; and
3. The chance to win exclusive prizes in regular competitions.

Interested? It takes less than a minute to sign up, just go to www.georgebellairs.com and your ebook will be sent to you.

Printed in Great Britain
by Amazon